Destiny's A Novel
HANDS

To Pastor Fred & Micki
Thank you for being our pastor
for these last months. I have so enjoyed
your sermons! Developing them into
Life Group notes was a pleasure. God bless you!
Violet Nesdoly

VIOLET NESDOLY

DESTINY'S HANDS
Copyright © 2012 by Violet Nesdoly

ISBN: 978-1-77069-452-1

Printed in Canada

Word Alive Press
131 Cordite Road, Winnipeg, MB R3W 1S1
www.wordalivepress.ca

Library and Archives Canada Cataloguing in Publication
Nesdoly, Violet, 1946-
    Destiny's hands / Violet Nesdoly.
ISBN 978-1-77069-452-1
    I. Title.
PS8627.E88D48 2012   C813'.6   C2011-908442-2

For my husband, Ernie.
*Without his love, encouragement, prayers, support,
and wonderful meals, this book would not exist.*

"For we are God's workmanship,
created in Christ Jesus to do good works,
which God prepared in advance for us to do."
—Ephesians 2:10

TABLE OF CONTENTS

AUTHOR'S NOTE

I have never thought of myself as a fiction writer. I don't daydream in stories. I never invented imaginary friends. I didn't entertain my school buddies with tales of Jim and Ann like my best friend did, or spin imaginary animal adventures to entertain my children.

Yet over the years certain characters have come to life for me. It seems to happen most often with historical figures. One such individual was the character Bezalel from the Bible, that craftsman of whom Moses said, *"See, the Lord has called by name Bezalel… and He has filled him with the Spirit of God, in wisdom and understanding, in knowledge and all manner of workmanship, to design artistic works...* " (Exodus 35:30–32, NKJV)

Who was this young man God filled with His Spirit for the arts? What was he like in his youth? Did he have any sense that he was special? What were his struggles and triumphs? *Destiny's Hands* is my fictional answer to those questions.

In addition to giving thanks to God, whose presence I have sensed throughout this project, I want to thank two special people who made unique contributions. Mary Lou Cornish read an earlier version of the story and challenged me to do better. I am so grateful for her critique and the ideas she offered. Charlie Van Gorkom explained the gold-working process to me in a way I could understand and explain. Thank you, Mary Lou and Charlie!

Hopefully this story and its characters will resonate with you at some level. To help with that, I've included a section of questions at the end of the book for use in personal reflection or book club discussion.

PROLOGUE

Ten-year-old Bezalel looked up from the striped pattern of reeds. He straightened his back and gazed into the pale midmorning sky. A long-necked ibis flapped above the reed beds. Nearby, a pair of squawking ducks rose in sudden flight. He rolled his shoulders and made a circular motion with his head to relax tense muscles, but the swish of reeds and faint tinkle of armbands warned him the overseer was nearby. He bent down again and resumed the endless rhythm— grasp the ridged stocks with his right hand, cut them with the knife in his left.

Onan followed close behind, picking up the cut stocks, stacking them in neat bundles, and tying them together. Someone would come later and carry the bundles out from the reed beds.

The day wore on and as the sun beat down hotter, Bezalel was thankful for the lukewarm water of the reed bed cooling his feet. At last the overseer's whistle signaled a break.

On the muddy bank, he drank the milk, ate the bread and tangy garlic paste his mother had packed, and felt revived. The others ate their lunches too. Then some of them skipped rocks across the surface of the river and challenged each other over whose rock would go the farthest. Onan and Reuben wrestled.

Bezalel sat slightly apart. He took up a twig and began to draw in the mud—the ibis standing in reeds, its long spindly neck, its sharp beak, and the solid silhouette of ducks in flight. He loved the soft surrender of the mud to his stick and its warm squish between his toes. He made a deep circle in the mud and dug out a chunk. He worked the ball, rolled it between his palms into a solid log, pressed and shaped it.

"Look, Bezalel is making a crocodile." Onan and Reuben came over and watched the animal take shape in his hands.

"It looks alive," said Reuben.

"How do you do that?" asked one of the stone-throwing boys who also stood and watched.

Bezalel shrugged. "I don't know."

"Did your father teach you?"

"No," said Bezalel. "My hands just know."

* * *

"I want one!" Zamri cried. "Dolls like Cetura, Anna, and Sephora have."

Noemi sighed in exasperation. Back from an exhausting day of cutting reeds, she now had to prepare the evening meal, straighten the house, and wash her family's clothes before finally sinking onto her mat for the night. She didn't have the energy to deal with one more request.

"I cannot make one today," she said. "You will have to wait. Soon I will have the time to gather the papyrus and weave one for you."

"Not a reed doll," Zamri said. "I want a doll with a face and drawing on it, just like Cetura's and Sephora's."

"Bezalel, get some papyrus chips for the stove," Noemi said. "Then go to the garden and get a cucumber and some chives."

Bezalel rose from the reed mat where he'd been resting. He too was tired from the day's work, but he went without complaint.

"Can I have a doll, please, please?" Zamri's voice rose in a childish whine.

"Oh, stop already. You have been rightly named the one who sings. Now please, stop your song."

Noemi made the meal. Just before it was time to eat, Uri came into the small hut. He too seemed exhausted. Only Zamri, intent on getting her doll, begged and chattered.

"Mother said she'd weave me one of papyrus, but I want one that has a face drawn on it, like the others. Can you make me one like that?"

Uri smiled indulgently at his five-year-old daughter. "Wait until your mother has time to make you a papyrus doll," he said, "and watch all your friends want one just like it."

After the meal, Bezalel went out. He didn't reappear until it was time for bed.

"Where have you been?" Noemi asked him when he appeared at the door.

"Just out, by the river," he said.

Zamri gave them no peace. Every evening, she hounded her mother. When would Noemi find time to make her a doll?

"Collect me the papyrus," Noemi said after Zamri reminded her again before she went off to work the fourth day running, "and I'll see what I can do tonight."

At suppertime, when Zamri took her place at the table, there was a papyrus-wrapped parcel at her spot.

"What is that?" Noemi asked.

"It's for Zamri," Bezalel said. When he smiled, there was a twinkle in his eye.

Noemi looked puzzled.

Just then, Zamri walked in. "You've made my doll!" she said to her mother.

"Open it," Noemi said. She looked as curious about the package as the little girl.

Zamri pushed apart the papyrus wrapping to reveal a doll—a clay doll with a beautifully drawn, detailed face. On its body were carved the outline of folds of cloth. It had the lifelike look of a swaddled infant. It was dry and hard.

"Where did you get that?" Noemi asked her son.

Bezalel smiled. "I made it."

His mother looked at him with both questioning and awe in her eyes. "Where did you learn to make something like that?"

He shrugged, looking self-conscious. "I don't know. I always draw in the mud, when we work on the riverbank."

Just then, Uri came in. Zamri ran to him with her new doll.

"Look, Papa, look! Bezalel made her!" She lifted her new treasure for him to inspect, then pulled it back and cradled the doll in her arms.

"Let's see," Uri said. Zamri carefully handed him the doll and he inspected it. He looked up and his eyes met Bezalel's. "Nice work, son. Did you have any help?"

Bezalel shook his head.

Uri looked at him thoughtfully. "You may just have worked your last day on the reed-gathering crew."

PART ONE

Slave

CHAPTER
one

BEZLALEL SMOOTHED GOLD OVER THE PLASTER SURFACE WITH HIS STONE stylus. How the foil transformed the statue from a nondescript ghostly beast to a glittering deity! No wonder they called gold the skin of the gods. They would name it Hathor after mounting it on a pedestal. Then they would bow low before it, offering bowls of grain and fruit, after which they would dance around it.

Out of the corner of his eye, he saw movement. How it caught his attention, he wasn't sure, for Pharaoh's goldsmith shop in Pi-Ramesses was a hive of activity. Yet he knew she was there again, Karem, hovering near the overseer Khafra, her father. Bezalel felt her black, kohl-rimmed eyes. They bored into him until he wished he could disappear.

He moved around the image so that the statue came between them. Maybe she would go away. But a minute later, she was beside him.

"It looks so real." Her voice sounded high and childish, a stark contrast to her bold almond eyes and the serious weight of hair that hung like an ebony carving, thick and shining, just above her shoulders. "How do you do it?"

He glanced into her face and thought again how much her eyes looked like a cat's.

"How do you do it?" she asked again. Her question sounded innocent, but Bezalel felt apprehensive. Why did she keep coming to him like this, singling him out? He cringed when he thought of the teasing that would come later.

"Will you teach me?" Her eyes were taunting now.

He didn't trust himself to look past her face, down to the sheer-pleated linen that outlined her form.

"Why don't you come to me? At the palms below the upper fountain?"

Bezalel felt his face go hot. She had never been so forward before. He didn't say anything but instead went around the image where he'd been working and kept on smoothing the gold.

She followed him. "Why are you ignoring me? You know that's dangerous. I can get you in trouble."

She was right, of course. Her father was the overseer. Bezalel glanced to where Khafra stood, watching them. Still Bezalel kept silent, until at last she left.

He looked around the shop. The workday was done. Other craftsmen and slaves were putting their tools away, covering their half-finished projects with cloths and leaving for home or the workers' encampment. He picked up his tools and placed them in their spot, covered the image, then walked out into the cool air of early evening.

His work-home at the encampment was a short walk from the shop. But tonight he found himself traveling past the craftsmen quarters, through the closing market, to the canal, over the bridge, and between the houses of the old town of Avaris. No matter that his body felt exhausted from hours of work. After his run-in with Karem, he yearned to be with his own people. He needed to feel the kindness of his mother Noemi, the stability of his father Uri, the fun and purity of his younger sister, fourteen-year-old Zamri, and most of all the solidity of Grandfather Hur.

Were those footsteps following him? Behind the sounds of coming and going all around him, the steady echo of his own steps seemed suddenly ominous. He darted between two houses and listened. They continued to get closer, then stopped. He waited for a long time, tense and motionless. Nothing. He must have imagined it.

He slipped back onto the street and quickened his pace through town, glancing back from time to time. No one. Finally he came to the city wall and the path that led to Goshen.

* * *

There was something different about Goshen today. Bezalel sensed it as he strode the clay path past the first huts of the settlement. People talked in animated groups of twos and threes. Children dodged in and out amongst the adults in laugh-filled games as if they had caught the excitement.

But even with this premonition, he was surprised when he saw the crowd at the meeting place. It was the elders, his grandfather's friends. In the twilight he recognized Aaron, Caleb, and Simeon. At the center of the crowd stood a striking man he had never seen before. He was dressed simply, like a shepherd with a dusty robe over a loose tunic. On his head was a cloth covering secured with a headband like desert travelers wore. His lined, tanned face looked like leather. Shaggy white hair poked out from under the head covering and a long, full beard framed that leather visage like a cloud. But there all ordinariness stopped, for from the face shone eyes that burned like embers. Who was this man?

Bezalel stood at the fringe of the crowd, listening as Aaron spoke.

"We met in the desert. This in itself is amazing, as I haven't seen or heard from him in forty years. God has given him a message and an assignment. You tell them, Moses."

Moses! This was the prince-turned-murderer whose name was legend among their people. Bezalel took another long look at the man. But he was just a shepherd and he looked so ancient, except for his fierce eyes.

Moses, who had been scanning the faces of the crowd, turned his attention to Aaron and shook his head. He spoke to his brother, who listened, and then, facing the crowd, projected his voice so all could hear. "Moses says, 'Aaron has agreed to be my voice. Listen to him as you would to me.'"

Moses spoke to Aaron again. Aaron listened and then continued. "It all started one very ordinary day when I was herding my flock on the back side of the desert. I noticed a bush. It was on fire. It was isolated and I wondered how the fire had started. I watched and then heard a voice, calling me near. 'Moses, Moses!' I answered, 'Here I am.'"

Aaron stopped to listen as Moses whispered to him. He then went on, repeating his brother's words.

"'Do not come any closer,' the voice said. 'Rather, take off your sandals, for the place where you stand is holy ground.'"

"Was there anyone around?" someone asked.

"No," said Moses. He spoke to Aaron again and Aaron continued.

"I knew it was the voice of Him. Elohim. And so I bared my feet and He talked to me from the bush. 'I am the God of your Fathers,' the voice said, 'the God of Abraham, the God of Isaac, and the God of Jacob.'"

"What did He look like?" someone called out.

Moses' eyes swept the onlookers until they found the questioner. He bored into the man with his gaze. "I did not look," he said. "Who could look on Him and live?"

Silence gripped the crowd as Moses continued to scan the onlookers, as if to confront anyone else who would question him on this. Then he spoke to Aaron again and Aaron continued.

"He told me He has not forgotten you. He has seen your misery and your crying out and your suffering. He will rescue you and bring you to a vast land flowing with milk and honey. To Canaan, the home of the Canaanites, Hittites, Amorites, Perizzites, Hivites, and Jebusites."

A murmur of amazement rose among the elders as Aaron repeated Moses' words. Gradually the volume increased until the shouts of "Praise Yahweh!" and "Hallelujah!" drowned out his voice.

"Elohim has heard our groaning!" someone shouted above the crowd. "Praises, praises!" Bezalel recognized his grandfather's voice.

"But how will it happen?" someone asked. "How will He free us?"

Moses spoke to Aaron again and his brother continued. "God says that Pharaoh will resist our attempts to gain freedom at first. It will take some time, but He will also prove His power with signs."

There was a moment of stillness. Then, with a flourish, Moses threw his staff onto the ground. A gasp rose up from the crowd. Those near him stepped backward, pushing into the people behind them, trampling on their feet.

"What is it?" asked those who couldn't see.

"A snake. It has turned into a snake!"

The next moment Moses bent down, grasped the tail of the snake, and it stiffened again into a staff. Another gasp went through the crowd.

With an elaborate and exaggerated motion, he hid his hand between his tunic and cloak. The crowd was silent and watched transfixed as, a minute later, he pulled the hand back out. It was shriveled, misshapen, and spotted with sores and scabs.

Again the people shrank from Moses. Leprosy!

Moses raised his hand, twisting it in all directions so everyone could see the dooming lesions, the crippling condition. Then he slipped it into his clothes again, left it there for a minute, and pulled it out.

It was whole—clean and sound.

Yet another gasp went up. "It is a miracle! God really is with us. He has remembered us."

Bezalel saw his grandfather Hur fall to his knees and raise his face and hands in voiceless worship. One by one, the other leaders and onlookers followed his example, some bending their faces to touch the ground, others lying prone.

Bezalel shrank back into the shadows but remained standing. Did they really think that an old desert shepherd—no matter what his reputation and how strong his magic—would convince Pharaoh to let them go? He had seen similar tricks done by Pharaoh's magicians.

He left the crowd and walked through the dark streets of Goshen to his family's home.

CHAPTER
two

Bezalel set out toward Pi-Ramesses in the predawn darkness the next morning, his mind replaying what he had seen last night. There was no question Moses had done some spectacular tricks. But were they enough to get the Israelites freed? Never!

Bezalel had told his father, mother, and Zamri what he had seen when he returned to the house. But it was Hur, who arrived shortly after, and his version of the story that got them dreaming about freedom. Now his family was excited about the prospect of no longer being slaves.

Bezalel had told them not to get their hopes up, though he didn't say outright what he thought of Yahweh. Did He even exist? His family prayed and prayed and nothing happened. The gentle pressure of his clothes against the amulet he wore reminded him of his allegiance. He now trusted in Ptah—the patron god of craftsmen. Khafra had given a charm to every worker and told them it was to Ptah their prayers should be directed, for he was the one on whom all craftsmen were dependent for their creative wisdom. Bezalel didn't even want to think what his family and Moses would make of that.

Maybe he should have told them about *his* freedom plan—how Khafra favored him and was giving him more and more responsibility. How it was only a matter of time before he would be a powerful craftsman in his own right. How he would one day build a beautiful house in the city, buy his family's freedom, and bring them all out of Goshen to live with him.

In the distance, Bezalel saw the walls of Pi-Ramesses glow in the sunrise. What a majestic and beautiful the city it was! His people had played a big part in building it. Pharaoh needed them for his projects. In fact, if Moses gave Pharaoh reason to suspect rebellion amongst the Hebrews, he might make things even worse for all of them. Pharaoh would never let them go.

He arrived at the shop, entered, collected his tools, and resumed the intricate work of covering the steer statue with gold, aware the whole while that Khafra was watching him.

* * *

"There will be a change of routine today," Khafra announced at a morning meeting of workers a few days later. "The Hebrews among us obviously do not have enough to do. So beginning today, each Hebrew must not only complete his work on time like before, but also find and deliver the materials for it."

There was a murmur amongst the slaves and craftsmen as they eyed their Hebrew companions with suspicion. They were easy to pick out with their hairy heads and full beards.

Could this be Moses' doing, Bezalel wondered? If so, he was making things worse, just as Bezalel had feared. Not only would the new demand impact how quickly he got his projects done, but it put him at odds with Khafra, whom he needed to impress. Bezalel felt the stares of questioning eyes, heavy with disapproval, as everyone went back to their jobs.

"Do you know the reason for this?" whispered Shoshan, an Israelite from the tribe of Reuben, when they met at the well that supplied water for the shop.

"Moses is back. I saw him when I was in Goshen a few days ago," said Bezalel. "He made the rash promise that he would free our people from slavery. It seems he may be stirring things up." Out of the corner of his eye, he saw Khafra barreling toward them.

"Bezalel. Shoshan. Back to work!"

The atmosphere in the workers' encampment had changed too. The hostility in the air was palpable as slaves and workers of other nationalities singled out the Hebrews for abuse.

"Hairy animals!"

"You should all go back to brickmaking!"

"What happened to master's pet?" scoffed one of Bezalel's Egyptian coworkers, who had often shown resentment when Khafra gave Bezalel special assignments.

* * *

"Moses has returned." Rahotep announced the news to Khafra in a voice heavy with meaning.

"Moses? The Hebrew who grew up as Pharaoh's child? The murderer?"

"The same," Rahotep said. "He and his brother, a common slave named Aaron, went before Pharaoh again today. They demanded our king let the Israelites go."

Rahotep, the overseer of all the guild workers, came often to chat with Khafra. He had arrived shortly before the noontime break this day, obviously excited. From where Bezalel was gilding the legs of the cow image, he strained to hear their conversation.

"Leave the country?" Khafra asked. "The nerve! They are ours. What would we do without their labor?"

"Exactly! Of course, Pharaoh would have none of it. Even though Moses performed magic. Threw his staff down and it turned into a snake. But our magicians could do it too. They won't escape with such tricks. By the way, how is the new policy working?"

"The workmen are definitely busier," said Khafra. "I've noticed a little chitchat between them, but nothing that could be called organized resistance. Give it some time. I'm sure these new constraints will keep the people out of mischief."

CHAPTER
three

Bezalel jogged toward his Goshen home in the late afternoon sun. He had finished the Hathor statue and Khafra had given him permission to visit his family. As he neared the house, his anticipation grew. His mother, father, sister, and grandfather were always so happy to see him. He imagined all of them sitting around the table eating his mother's fragrant stew and bread, catching up on each other's lives. He could hardly wait.

But when he arrived, there was no smell of cooking in the house. His mother, though she gave him a hug, seemed preoccupied, her forehead creased in a permanent frown.

"I'm so tired," she said as she caught him glancing at the cooking fire embers that waited to be revived. "Since Pharaoh has made us get our own straw, there's been no end of work. We're all very weary."

Father was also quiet and seemed distracted. He was the Israeli overseer of a brickmaking crew and had to enforce this law on his workers. Bezalel could imagine the complaints he was hearing.

He should have expected this, for if the situation was tense for him in Khafra's shop, where he was as much an apprentice as a slave, it was bound to be worse for those who were in full-fledged bondage.

Only Grandfather seemed unmoved in his hope. "There will come a time when this will all work out," he said later as the family gathered for the meal. "Moses is a messenger from God. He told us that Yahweh has heard us and will answer our prayers."

His simple faith irritated Bezalel. Did he actually believe what he said?

After the meal, when Bezalel was helping his mother and Zamri with the cleanup, he heard voices in the courtyard. A minute later, Uri appeared where they were working. "Moses will be speaking shortly in the public square. We must go hear him."

The family joined hundreds of others as they trooped toward Goshen's meeting place.

Moses and Aaron stood on a raised platform that someone had constructed so they could be seen above the crowd. Bezalel saw that today Moses didn't look as assured and confident as he had the first time. Again he talked through Aaron, one sentence at a time spoken softly to his brother, who then spoke it aloud to the people.

"I see that you're discouraged and tired. I've gone to Yahweh about it. I've asked Him what to say to you."

There was silence, though Bezalel sensed, looking at the surly expressions around him, that the people weren't nearly as receptive as they had been when Moses first arrived.

Moses continued, "God told me to say, 'I am the Lord. I will bring you out from under the yoke of the Egyptians. And I will free you from being slaves to them.'"

Despite the stirring words, Bezalel heard mutterings around him.

"Sure, sure..." said a man on his right, his voice heavy with sarcasm.

"That's what you said last time," someone shouted.

"What other fantastic promises do you have for us?" came from someone else.

The brothers carried on, ignoring the mockery. "God says I will redeem you with an outstretched arm and with mighty acts of judgment."

"Show us your next move then!" interrupted another voice from the crowd.

"But don't put yourself out!"

As the naysayers gained volume, Aaron raised his voice. "Listen to what Yahweh says: 'I will take you as My own people and I will be your God and then you will know that I am the Lord your God who brought you out from under the yoke of the Egyptians. And I will bring you to the land I swore with uplifted hand to give to Abraham, to Isaac, and to Jacob. I will give it to you as a possession: I am the Lord.'"

"Why are we listening to this when we could be sleeping and regaining our strength for tomorrow?" shouted a loud voice from the crowd. A spattering of agreement followed as people clapped and shouted "Hear! Hear!" With that, they began leaving for home, still muttering and complaining.

Bezalel trudged home with his family. When they reached the house, his mother stumbled at the door. He caught her before she fell.

"I'm sorry, but I'm so tired I can hardly raise my feet," she said. "I don't know if I can stand much more of this."

Uri put his arm around her. "I know. It's tough," he said as he helped her to a cushion on the floor.

But Hur was immovable in his optimism. "God will see us through this. I know the God of Moses. He is my God too. He will bring us through this difficult time. Just have faith."

Bezalel rarely challenged his grandfather, but today he couldn't suppress his nagging thoughts. "How can you say that?" he asked. "Moses' demands are just making things worse, for you and for us in Pi-Ramesses too."

"Sometimes God's ways are hard to understand," replied Hur. "Look at how He dealt with our father Abraham, giving him the best land over Lot's when it looked like the worst."

"But this is now," Bezalel said. "Our people have been slaves for hundreds of years. If you think Moses will convince Pharaoh to let us go free by doing a few magic tricks, you don't know Pharaoh. But listen, if you give me time, I may be able to help you."

"You?" Uri looked puzzled

"Yes, me. My overseer Khafra often shows me favor. In the time I've worked for him, he has given me much responsibility. Soon I will have influence. Then I will build a house for you in Pi-Ramesses. I will buy your freedom and you can live with me."

"You surely are talented," Hur said. "But I don't believe Yahweh gave you your skill to serve the Egyptians and their gods."

"Yahweh?" said Bezalel. He hated it when Grandpa Hur gave Yahweh credit for everything. He had no understanding of how things really worked. Throwing caution aside, he went on. "My skill and knowledge comes from Ptah, who fashioned the universe and who helps all craftsmen." He pulled down his tunic at the neck to show the gold amulet he wore—a horned bull with a sun disk on its head.

"Ptah!" Hur's face went pale and his eyes grew large in horror. "Never! You are Bezalel. Have you forgotten the meaning of your name? 'In the Shadow and Protection of El,' the God of Israel."

Bezalel felt his heart pound. He had never talked to Grandpa Hur like this before. Still, he was determined to make his point. "I don't know El," he said. "He has never done anything for me. Neither have you seen Him. How do you know He even exists?" His voice shook in spite of his bold words.

"You don't know what you say," said Hur. "It is He who created you with the wisdom and skill to make things. You will discover that He is real, and He is the only one to serve."

Bezalel didn't answer him, though in his heart he doubted it very much.

* * *

When Bezalel returned to work two days later, he saw that the situation had grown tenser than before. Tempers flared as supplies ran short and Egyptian craftsmen were kept waiting while the Hebrews scrambled to complete their parts of joint projects. Bezalel was determined not to let the friction bother him. He would make Khafra see that he could handle whatever came his way. Now that he had told his family his plan, he had to prove to them that he could follow through with it.

His new assignment was to help with a set of chairs for the Pharaoh. The legs and arms needed to be carved. The backs would have cloisonné inlays. Khafra first gave him the task of designing the inlay pattern. He decided to use green feldspar and orange carnelian in a lotus pattern.

After Khafra supplied him with the dimensions of the chairs, Bezalel spent a good while figuring out how much wood, gold leaf, and flux he would need. He enjoyed working with numbers and making calculations.

After he had worked it all out, he gave his plans and the list of materials to Khafra, who checked it and handed it to a scribe to copy onto an official order document for the storehouse. As soon as Bezalel received it back, he walked the fifteen minutes to the storehouse to begin collecting his supplies.

He picked out sycamore fig wood with a beautiful grain. He lingered over the precious stones, clawing through them until he found the most perfect specimens. Next he found the rolls of gold leaf, flux, and other materials for the inlay. He set everything aside in a pile. When he had collected it all, he brought it to one of the scribes who accounted for each item and matched it with Khafra's order.

Then he had the laborious job of transporting everything to the shop on his own. He made one trip after another and was soon hot and tired. He needed a drink!

After he had taken the final trip, he took his clay mug to the well. The cold water would taste so good, he thought as he drew out the bucket and poured the refreshing liquid into his cup—and gasped. The water was red as blood. And it smelled.

"What's wrong with this water?" he cried out.

Violet Nesdoly

The others crowded around to look. Khafra hurried over. No one knew what had happened. Someone else had poured a drink only a few minutes before and it had been fine.

"We have some extra water stored in jugs and jars along the wall here," said Khafra. "Take a drink from one of those."

Bezalel filled his cup with water from a jug, but it too was red and foul. He dumped it out. Of course, now that he couldn't drink his thirst was even more intense.

Various workers supplied reasons as to what could be wrong. But one thing was certain—the water was undrinkable. And how were they going to last all day without a drink? Someone walked down to the river and came back with the news that it too was red, as was the canal and the lake. The red water was everywhere. That night, Bezalel and everyone in the slave encampment went to bed thirsty.

It wasn't until the next day that someone discovered that if you dug down past the topsoil and reached ground water, it came up clear. Khafra sent a slave from the shop to join the hundreds of others digging for water along the riverbank. He brought a jug of this precious ground water to the workshop and the workers were each given a small ration of water for the day.

* * *

Bezalel was beginning to carve the chair legs when Rahotep came in and walked over to where he and Khafra usually talked. Bezalel busied himself with his work but strained to hear Rahotep describe what he had seen the day before.

"Pharaoh had just risen. He was out welcoming the sun when this Moses and Aaron accosted him. Again they demanded that he let the Israelites go. Of course, our noble king would never hear of that. Then Moses said, 'Remember the staff that I used the other day, that changed into a snake? If you don't let my people go, I'll strike the water of the Nile and it will change into blood. The fish will die and the river will stink. The Egyptians won't be able to drink.'"

Bezalel felt a pang of alarm. Moses again. Could it be that he had more magic at his disposal than he had shown on the day of his arrival?

"Of course our Pharaoh held firm," Rahotep continued. "So Moses told Aaron to stretch his staff over the water, which he did. That's when everything turned red. You should see the fish along the water's edge. They're coming up all over and they're dead and stinking. This bloody water is everywhere—blood in the water pots, blood in the jugs. There's even blood in the cooking pots. But when someone discovered there was clean water if one dug past the surface, our Pharaoh's magicians were able to change that to blood with their scepters. So, you see, our magicians' magic is just as powerful as the magic of these Israelites."

Bezalel felt oddly reassured by the fact that Pharaoh's magicians could duplicate Moses' tricks. Surely a shepherd with a rod could not defeat the Egyptian gods!

CHAPTER

four

BEZALEL PUT DOWN HIS TOOLS, STRETCHED, AND ROLLED HIS SHOULDERS, flexing the muscles, tense from the cramped position in which he did the intricate carvings. Despite the physical strain on his body, he loved his work. He enjoyed releasing the chair legs from the shapeless wood. He looked forward to making the arms and the back, watching the decorative parts he had imagined take shape under his hands, positioning the gemstones in interlocking mosaic patterns and fixing them in place. He was energized by the busy workshop. When he was absorbed in his work, time evaporated like morning mist on the Nile.

But now the day was getting hotter by the minute and he needed another drink. Thankfully, after a week of drinking muddy ground water, the well was clean and fresh again.

Bezalel got to the well just as Shoshan was drawing up the bucket. He watched as his friend poured water into his cup, but jumped back as a frog sprang from the bucket and landed beside his foot.

Shoshan stopped pouring and peered into the bucket. "Three more!" he exclaimed, dropping the bucket with a clatter as the reptiles leaped into the air.

Workmen gathered around. One of them lowered the bucket back into the well to draw fresh water, but it came up with more frogs wiggling and jumping onto the well's edge, flinging themselves at arms, feet, and the floor.

Khafra came over. "What's the commotion?" he asked. "Get back to work."

"Frogs everywhere," someone said.

"Don't joke," Khafra said. Then he wheeled the bucket down and pulled it up. There were even more frogs than before. They writhed in the bucket, then sprang from it and hopped across the shop floor.

At first they were a source of fun as workers trapped them with hands and tools, dodged their leaps, and sprang them on each other. However, as they kept landing on arms, necks, and heads, jumping from the floor, crawling up legs, and getting in the way of work, they became pests.

"What's going on?" they asked each other.

Moses is probably behind this too, Bezalel thought to himself.

Later that day, when Rahotep made his usual visit to the shop, Bezalel's suspicions were confirmed.

"It was Moses and Aaron again," Rahotep said to Khafra. "They went to Pharaoh and demanded that Pharaoh let the people go so they could worship their God. They said if Pharaoh refused to let them go, he would plague the country with frogs. Then Aaron took Moses' staff and held it out while he turned in a circle. Minutes later, frogs started appearing from every wet place. Mind you, our magicians were able to do the same thing. But now we're stuck with these horrible pests and they're everywhere. How will we get rid of them?"

As Rahotep was talking, Karem ran up. She stood beside her father, silent until Rahotep was finished. On seeing her, Bezalel busied himself with his job, making sure he didn't catch her eye.

"Is this your daughter?" Rahotep asked. "She has become quite the young woman."

"Yes, this is Karem," Khafra replied. "Do you want something?"

"Can you come home?" Karem said. "There are frogs everywhere. They came out of the pond in our courtyard. They're even in the jugs and pots in the kitchen, jumping into the dough in the cook's kneading bowl."

"It's that vile Moses," Rahotep replied. "He is disrupting everything. He demands that the Hebrew slaves be freed so they can worship their God. He is bringing these plagues on us."

"Hebrews? Who are they?" Karem asked.

"Shoshan is a Hebrew," said someone.

"And Benjamin," said another.

"Bezalel," said someone else.

Bezalel ducked his head when he heard his name, but Karem had spotted him and an instant later was standing in front of him.

"What God do you worship that sends these frogs? Can He make them go away?"

"I don't know," mumbled Bezalel. He hated that he had been implicated in these events and connected in any way to Moses. But it seemed he couldn't avoid it.

"Eek!" Karem shrieked as a frog hopped onto her foot and another came flying through the air to hit her hand. "Where can I go to get away from these horrible frogs?"

"I don't have time to deal with the frog problem at home now," her father said. "I'll see what I can do later."

Karem left the shop with mincing steps and eyes lowered so as to avoid stepping on the leaping reptiles. Bezalel took a deep breath of relief.

* * *

The frogs lasted for days. Even though the workers killed all those they caught, new frogs kept appearing. Then, just as quickly as they came, they began dying. Bezalel found he had to watch where he stepped to keep from slipping on their slimy remains.

The slaves whose job it was to keep the shop clean made piles of their carcasses. But they obviously didn't find them all because in the heat of the day the shop began to smell horribly of decay. Bezalel tied a cloth over his nose so he didn't have to breathe in the putrid stench.

On his daily visit, Rahotep told Khafra how the plague had come to an end.

"Pharaoh was beside himself over the frogs," he said. "Two days ago, he called for Moses and Aaron and begged them to pray to their God to remove them."

Khafra grunted.

"That Moses so revolts me," Rahotep went on. "You should have heard how disrespectfully he spoke to our Pharaoh: 'I leave *you* the honor of setting the time for me to pray for the end of the frogs.' Pharaoh replied, 'Tomorrow,' and wouldn't you know it, yesterday they began dying. Of course, Moses and Aaron were back today demanding Pharaoh release the Hebrew slaves in exchange for getting rid of them."

"Pharaoh didn't give in, did he?" Khafra asked.

"Of course not. But I'd suggest you keep a very close eye on your Hebrews. Something is definitely brewing among them."

Rahotep's last words echoed in Bezalel's head. Was there a chance Moses really could unite the Hebrew people and lead them to freedom with these signs?

His thoughts were interrupted by something crawling up his legs, over his torso, and across his arms. He looked down to see a cloud that looked like dust from the shop floor. It caught the light like chaff from the winnowers at harvest time. But instead of drifting away like chaff, the particles clung to every part of his body. Gnats!

CHAPTER
five

THE GNATS LASTED A GOOD WEEK. FINALLY THEY DISAPPEARED, ONLY TO be replaced by flies. Flies were everywhere. They bit arms, legs, and faces. They crawled over food, fell into the water, squeezed between skin and clothing, and got tangled in Bezalel's beard. His constant need to swat them interfered with his work.

Everyone in the shop was short-tempered and the suspicious attitude toward the Hebrew workers increased. Fellow craftsmen who had formerly chatted easily with Bezalel now avoided his work area. At the workers' encampment, the camaraderie with other workers was gone. Bezalel, who had once shared his sleeping space with a Nubian and an Edomite, found himself deserted. He moved his mat near Shoshan and other Hebrews.

One afternoon, when the flies had been with them for many days, Rahotep came again. After his usual inspection of the shop, he lingered to talk with Khafra.

"I predict that tomorrow the flies will disappear," he said.

"How can you say that?" asked Khafra.

"Because Moses came today," Rahotep said. "He has convinced Pharaoh to let the Israelites go. Moses insisted they take a three-day journey into the desert to offer sacrifices to his God, and Pharaoh said, 'I will let you go to offer your sacrifices. Just pray for me.' So Moses said, 'As soon as I leave you, I will pray to the Lord, and tomorrow the flies will leave. Only be sure that you keep your promise and actually let the people go. Don't break it again.'"

This news filled Bezalel with dismay. In a matter of weeks Moses, had been way more successful at wearing down Pharaoh's resistance than he had ever thought possible. What about his family? If Moses freed the people, would they leave him behind in Egypt? He had never considered that possibility before, but now the fact that it could happen hit him full force.

His work had always been the most important thing to him. But the thought of being left alone in Egypt made him realize his family was important to him too—perhaps more important than he had realized. Was it possible that Moses was actually going to free the Israelites tomorrow? If so, he needed to be with his family.

Though he wasn't due for a visit to Goshen for at least another week, he decided to take the long trek that night. Besides, with suspicion of the Israelites growing, who knew when visits to Goshen would be forbidden altogether?

As he made his way through the market, he felt again like he was being followed. But why? And by whom? He increased his pace and kept glancing over his shoulder. When the crowd thickened, he stepped off the path between two buildings, hoping to give his follower the slip. He waited a good while, then stepped into the crowd again.

Almost too late, he caught sight of Nefti, a burly servant of Khafra's. The man was standing some distance ahead, surveying the crowd as if looking for someone. In the second before he looked Bezalel's way, Bezalel hunched over, covered his head with his robe, and changed his walk to an exaggerated limp. His heart pounded as he passed the place where Nefti stood. Would the man recognize him? And why would Khafra send Nefti to spy on him anyway?

He walked like this for a long while, not daring to check if anyone was behind him. When the crowd thinned, he finally straightened up and looked around. Nefti was nowhere to be seen.

Flies still buzzed around him as he jogged along the canal, puzzling over what had just happened. He swatted them away from his sweating face. It was hard to believe these pests would actually be gone tomorrow, as Rahotep had said.

However, the closer he got to Goshen, the fewer flies there were. As he strode along the hard clay path, taking the final steps toward home, he realized there were no flies. The plague was over even before the day Moses had promised.

He looked around for signs that the people were preparing to leave but saw that life was going on pretty much as it always had. He had been worried for nothing.

Bezalel's family was delighted to see him. They seemed in much better spirits than last time. His mother's eyes had regained their sparkle. "What a wonderful surprise," she said, leaving her cooking pot to give him a hug.

Zamri was her usual bubbly self. "Look what I made," she said, holding up a tunic for Bezalel to inspect. "Sephora's mother is teaching us to make clothes."

Even Father joined in the conversation without getting the usual distracted look in his eyes that told Bezalel he was absorbed in weightier matters.

They shared their stories of coping with the blood water, frogs, and gnats.

"But these flies were the worst thing so far," Bezalel said.

Noemi looked at him, puzzled. "What flies?"

"The swarms that have tormented us for at least a week," Bezalel replied.

"We haven't had flies," Noemi said.

"What? In Pi-Ramesses we were going mad with them. In fact, as a result of them, I overheard that Pharaoh has agreed to let us go with Moses. That's why I had to come home tonight." Bezalel told them of the latest conversation between Rahotep and Khafra.

"That's the best news I've heard since Moses returned," Hur spoke up from his place at the table. "I told you we should be making our preparations to leave." Then, looking straight at Bezalel, he asked, "What do you make of Yahweh now? Do you still question whether He is real?"

Bezalel looked away from his grandfather's strong gaze. He didn't know what to say, for that same question had come to him more than once in the last weeks.

Uri shook his head in amazement. "I must admit I never thought I'd see the day."

For Hur, Noemi, and Uri, the dream of leaving Egypt and the slave life had always glistened like an impossible-to-reach oasis somewhere off in the distance. Now that there was even the slimmest chance of it coming to pass, the thought of being free seemed beyond wonderful.

The family talked late into the night as they spun what-ifs and made plans that were half-practical, half-outlandish.

For the first time in his life, Bezalel let himself get swept away by their talk of freedom. "We would need some kind of shelter to live in," he said. "Wherever we end up, there will be traveling first."

"Our forefathers knew how to make tents out of hides," said Hur. "I'll see if I can find someone who remembers."

"Would we take the animals?" asked Zamri. She had hand-fed a lamb and named it Curls. Bezalel knew she would never willingly be separated from it.

"Moses would make sure we took everything," Uri said. "We need our animals to sacrifice to God, in any case."

"What does that mean?" asked Zamri.

"Our God Yahweh is holy and terrible," said Hur, looking straight at Bezalel. "We bring Him the most precious thing when we come to Him. Not chanted prayers and grain, food, or treasure like the Egyptians sacrifice to their images. We bring Him a life. When Yahweh sees the blood and smells the smoke of the animal offered on the altar—a lamb or a calf or a pigeon—He accepts us and hears our prayers."

This time Bezalel listened attentively and without arguing. After all of Moses' signs, perhaps there was something to Grandpa's Yahweh after all. He covered his tunic with his robe, careful to hide the shape of the bulky amulet in its folds.

* * *

Bezalel busied himself with the chairs. He was in the process of carving the arms and still had much to do. The decorative sections needed to be finished. The carnelian and feldspar inlay had to be assembled and melded into place. This was one of his favorite parts of the project and he left it to the end, when everything else was almost complete. After all the pieces were made, he would drill holes and fit them together to assemble the furniture.

As he concentrated on making each arm piece like the others, his hands were sure and skilled. His pulse quickened as he noticed Khafra's eyes on him again, watching the designs take shape under his chisel. The overseer's gaze made him nervous.

When he looked up again, Khafra's attention was elsewhere. Bezalel let his mind wander back to the previous night and his visit home. Would Pharaoh ever let them go, or would he keep promising then changing his mind as he had in the past?

* * *

For about a week, life in the shop was like it had been before Moses had returned. Then one day Khafra didn't come to the shop all day.

Word circulated amongst the workers and slaves that there was trouble with the cattle.

That night at the slave encampment, Bezalel heard that all the cattle—the cows, sheep, and goats—were dying of some mysterious disease. Khafra's son was one of Pharaoh's agricultural overseers. There were rumors that Khafra had gone to Pharaoh to plead for mercy for his son.

Bezalel wondered about Goshen. Had this strange cattle disease struck them too? Or had it missed them, like the flies? He hoped with all his heart they had been spared. He couldn't imagine Zamri's grief at finding Curls had died.

When Khafra returned to work several days later, he was quiet and preoccupied. More than once, Bezalel looked up to catch his overseer's eyes fixed on him. Was Khafra angry or watching to catch him in a mistake?

When Rahotep came on his regular inspection, he asked Khafra about his son.

"Hathor be thanked, Pharaoh has not punished him," Khafra said.

"He shouldn't," said Rahotep. "It was Moses again. And Pharaoh much appreciates the tip you gave to check on Goshen. He sent his servants to do that. It seems none of their cattle have died. Still, our king in his god-like wisdom refuses to let these Israelites go."

Bezalel's relief at hearing Goshen's livestock had been spared was tinged with discouragement because of Pharaoh's determination to keep them in Egypt. His family would be so disappointed. For the first time in his life, he felt the same way. Their joyous talk of freedom the other night had awakened something new in him.

CHAPTER

six

BEZALEL CHISELED OUT THE INLAY SECTIONS OF THE CHAIR WITH SHARP, angry strokes. He was annoyed with Khafra, who had just come by and ordered him to redesign a part of his project even though Bezalel had thought it through to the last detail and knew he had it right. He didn't like it when someone meddled in his designs, even when that someone was as skilled as Khafra.

And so he felt smug satisfaction when Rahotep made his regular visit and Bezalel overheard the latest palace gossip.

"Moses and Aaron were back again today," Rahotep told Khafra. Rahotep wore an unusual long-sleeved cloak. On his face and neck were several bandages.

"More antics?" asked Khafra.

"Oh yes. Of course they made their customary demand that Pharaoh let the Israelites go. And of course Pharaoh said no. So then both of them dipped their hands in a bucket of black dust they had brought with them, fine like soot, and tossed it into the air."

Khafra grimaced at the unlikely scene. "What was the meaning of that?"

"I'm not sure," said Rahotep. "But I do know that within the hour, servants who were attending Pharaoh were scratching welts which grew bigger by the minute. In fact, most of the palace staff seems to have come down with sores. When Pharaoh called for his magicians, they arrived with faces, arms, and legs dotted with them. Pharaoh asked them to intercede to Imhotep, but this seems beyond even him, for our god of medicine gave them neither the power to duplicate the sign nor brought them any relief from the pain and itching. Even I seem to have succumbed."

Rahotep drew open his cloak and Bezalel heard Khafra's sharp intake of breath.

"Maybe that explains this," Khafra said as he raised his tunic, something he customarily wore only in the coldest weather. From where he stood, Bezalel saw angry red patches all over his chest.

Just then, Karem entered the shop. She was carrying a cat in her arms and seemed distraught.

"Something is wrong with Bas," she said, her high-pitched childish voice choked with tears. "She won't eat or drink and keeps licking her fur. See, she's covered with sores."

She held the wriggling animal tight as she stroked against the grain of the cat's fur, revealing what was beneath.

Khafra inspected the cat's skin. "She has the same sores as we do," he said to Rahotep. He turned to Karem. "You'd better put her down, or you'll get them too."

"I think I already have," she said, holding the cat tight with one arm and lifting her heavy bangs with the other to reveal her forehead.

Bezalel didn't look. He couldn't take the chance of drawing her attention and having her come over to make another scene. But her father must have seen something, for Khafra said in a quiet, urgent tone, "Get home and bandage your skin. You don't want to be seen like that."

As the day wore on, more and more workers complained of itchiness and broke out in lumps that burned, pained, festered, and came to heads in pussy pimples and boils. Bezalel kept looking at his arms and legs, but there was not a mark on them. By the end of the day, however, every person in the shop was infected except for Bezalel, Shoshan, Benjamin, and the other Israelites.

The next morning, Bezalel arrived to find the carefully assembled inlay sections for the chair backs smashed in pieces on the floor. The sabotage was obviously connected to resentment toward the Hebrews and their immunity from the boils, for Shoshan's tools were missing and Benjamin's project had disappeared altogether. When Khafra found Bezalel crawling around, trying to salvage the gemstones, he looked disgusted and refused to listen to Bezalel's explanation of what had happened. Instead he cursed him for his carelessness and cancelled his next visit home to Goshen.

* * *

Past sky-blue fields of blossoming flax and waving barley heads, Bezalel jogged to his Goshen home. Cattle, sheep, and goats grazed in the pastures. He wondered where the farmers had gone to replenish their livestock after they had all been wiped out.

It had been weeks since he'd seen his family. They would wonder why he had been away so long. Did they still hold onto their dreams of freedom? He hoped so, though to him freedom didn't seem any closer than when he had last seen them.

His family was full of questions about what had kept him away. After Noemi's leek and lentil stew, they talked about their last time together when leaving Egypt had seemed like an any-day possibility.

"How do the people feel about Moses and what has been happening?" Bezalel asked.

"For the people in Goshen, life goes on normally," said Uri. "Almost everyone has become accustomed to the extra workload. But I hear from others like you that the pressure mounts in the cities."

"Things aren't like they used to be," Bezalel said. He told them of the attitude of the other workers and how the atmosphere at the shop had become toxic toward the Israelites. "Although I still enjoy my work, things can't go on like this. It seems to me that events are building to some sort of a climax."

That night, as Bezalel looked toward Pi-Ramesses, he saw storm clouds hovering over the city. In the night, he woke to the sound of wind and thunder. He got up to look and in the distance saw flashes of lightning. When he went back to sleep, sounds of thunder, wind, and rain were part of his dreams. In the morning, Goshen was sunny but clouds still hung over Pi-Ramesses, where lightning flashed and thunder rumbled well past midday.

The scene of the countryside as he neared the city the following morning shocked him. Where two days ago the blooming flax had been a reflection of the sky and barley heads had waved like ribbons in the wind, now the fields were a trampled desolation. They looked as if some giant beast had lain on them and pressed them flat.

A hush came over the workers in the shop when Bezalel entered. He squirmed under their hostile looks.

"What happened?" he asked, pausing beside Shoshan. "It looked from home like you had a terrible storm last night."

"Terrible isn't the word for it," said Shoshan. "It was the scariest thing I've ever lived through. You should see the encampment. The roof blew off in places. Good thing Khafra made us sleep in here."

"He let you sleep in the shop?"

"Yep. Told us we had no choice. Not everyone was like that. The hail hurt many of the ones who spent the night there. Some were even killed. Did it storm in Goshen?"

"Wind and rain," said Bezalel, "but no thunder and lightning. Certainly no hail."

Khafra entered the shop just then and the men scattered to their workstations. He looked unusually dour and stern.

"Terrible storm the last two days," Rahotep said as he entered the shop. He glanced around. "Looks like all your people survived."

"Yes," said Khafra. "I had them sleep here. I know enough about Moses and his predictions to take them seriously. Not like my fool son. I warned him to bring Pharaoh's herds under cover, but did he listen? No. Now all the cattle he just bought are dead—pummeled by ice. I fear Pharaoh will have his head."

"That's bad," said Rahotep. "If it's any consolation, Pharaoh has decided not to go through with yesterday's promise to let the Israelites go."

"I'm beginning to wonder whether that's such a good thing," Khafra said. "Is the devastation of Egypt worth it?"

CHAPTER
seven

"Zamri, bring me the platter for meat and the sauce bowls. Bezalel, make sure the cushions are plumped and the table ready for food." Noemi's face flushed as she made the last preparations for the meal. Bezalel was on a two-day visit home. Tonight, Moses was eating with them. Hur, who had been boyhood friends with Aaron, had invited him.

When their guest arrived, they sat down, Uri asked a blessing, and they began eating. But even the delicious roast lamb and bread dipped in savory sauces wasn't enough to distract Bezalel from their guest. He couldn't help but stare at the man with his wild white hair, full beard, lined face, and dark penetrating eyes. What could he see, Bezalel wondered? Did he know people's thoughts? Did he know about the Egyptian god Bezalel wore on his own person? Thankfully, Moses didn't look at him much. He seemed more interested in talking with Hur.

In answer to Hur's questions about his methods and why deliverance was taking so long, Moses answered without hesitation, yet Bezalel detected a defensive note in his voice: "I don't have to apologize for Yahweh," Moses said. "He has His own reasons for hardening Pharaoh's heart, for taking His time. Yahweh has told me that."

Then the old man closed his eyes and spoke as if remembering God's exact words to him. "Go to Pharaoh, for I have hardened his heart and the hearts of his officials so that I may perform these miraculous signs of Mine among them. That you may tell your children and grandchildren how I dealt harshly with the Egyptians and how I performed My signs among them and that you may know that I am the Lord."

Was he saying that these signs were as much to convince the Israelites of Yahweh's power as to trouble the Egyptians? Because they certainly had opened *his* eyes. He had heard the stories of Abraham, Isaac, Jacob, and Joseph as tales told by a work-weary mother at the end of an exhausting day. But to see Yahweh's power firsthand was altogether different, especially since he had identified so closely with the glittering gods of the Egyptians.

"There will be more signs," Moses said to them as he took his leave. "Pharaoh is no match for Yahweh. If you are wise, you will begin to prepare for the journey out of Egypt."

The next morning, as Bezalel jogged along the canal in the early morning moonlight, his mind dwelled on the things Moses had said. If he had any doubts that Yahweh was behind the unusual events in Egypt, the previous night had destroyed those. Yahweh's words to Moses seemed too knowing. They revealed a keen, insightful intelligence behind everything that was happening. "That you may know that I am the Lord," Moses had said.

The more he thought about it, the more uneasy he felt about his trust in Ptah. It had made perfect sense before Moses came, but now the gold image pressing into his skin felt foreign and heavy.

He had been so deep in thought that he was surprised to find he was already in the city. As he jogged past the Temple of Seth, he saw the priests entering, fresh from their purifying bath in the lake. The white-clad figures passed between the grand painted columns, so confident in the part they played in ushering in the new day and preserving the order that was rooted in Pharaoh's deity. If Yahweh was really the Lord, did that mean He was greater than all this? The closer Bezalel came to the shop, the more he sensed the pull of Egypt. How could he leave all this behind?

On the other hand, how could he live apart from his family?

At the shop, he collected his tools, then stood back and looked at his work with a critical eye. Here and there he made small adjustments to the carving. Then he picked up the mallet and roll of gold leaf. Now to make the chairs fit for a king.

He was absorbed in his work and didn't notice Rahotep come in. But his ears perked up as Rahotep and Khafra began discussing Moses and Aaron's latest visit.

"They are getting very demanding and disrespectful to our Lord," Rahotep said. "This morning, Moses had the nerve to say to him, repeating the words of his God, 'How long will you refuse to humble yourself before Me?'"

Khafra looked genuinely shocked. "Those Hebrews said that to Pharaoh?"

"There's more," replied Rahotep. "Now they're threatening locusts. They are to arrive tomorrow. Moses warned that they would clean up all that is left alive after the hail."

"Like the wheat and spelt," said Khafra.

"And our gardens. Everything that was under cover from the hail. But your question the other day, asking whether these pathetic people are worth the devastation of Egypt, got me thinking. Others are thinking along these lines too. A group of us prevailed on Pharaoh to call Moses and Aaron back. I think he's going to change his mind and let them go."

As Bezalel heard that last bit, his heart pounded and he broke into a sweat. Was Pharaoh really going to let them go at last? What should he do?

That night, a powerful wind disturbed Bezalel's sleep. He kept dreaming that his family was leaving, but one thing or another kept him from joining them.

The next morning, Bezalel had his answer as to what Pharaoh's decision had been. Despite the advice of his governors, he had obviously chosen locusts over freeing the slaves. The pathway from the slave encampment to the shop was jumping with them. They were everywhere, chewing on grass, eating the leaves off shrubs, disfiguring the fruit, leaping blindly and hitting his hands, chest, and face.

At midday, Karem came into the shop. "Father," she cried, "there are locusts everywhere. They've wrecked the garden, eaten the figs, the grapes, the cucumbers, the melons. Everything is gone. Why are these horrible things happening?"

"Hush, my dear," said Khafra. "Who knows what or who is behind this. It might just be fate, or a string of bad luck. Or maybe our priests have displeased the gods. Or perhaps it is as our priests say—the magic of Yahweh, the God of the Hebrews."

"Hebrews like Bezalel?" she asked. She marched over, stood in front of Bezalel, and spoke in a high, plaintive voice loud enough for everyone to hear. "Your God is mean and horrible. I thought you were a nice man. I like the things you make. But I don't like your God."

Bezalel's face reddened under her tirade. He couldn't help but hear the murmur of agreement that passed through the fellow workers. Karem now stood before him, waiting for an answer.

Usually he would have remained silent, but today he felt an argument rise in him. He looked at Karem more directly than he had ever done before and said, quietly, "Why don't you blame Pharaoh? He's the one who refuses to let my people go."

For a second, there was shocked silence in the shop. Bezalel shot an apprehensive glance at Khafra.

Khafra seemed unmoved. "What are you all gawking at?" he said, breaking the silence. "Get back to work."

Bezalel busied himself with the mallet and gold, though his mind was in turmoil. What had he just said? How could he stay here any longer? But when could he leave, and how?

That evening, as he was tidying his workspace, Khafra, who had left earlier, returned. Bezalel felt a cringe of fear as his overseer stood next to him.

"Young man. Bezalel…" Khafra seemed unusually hesitant, even uncomfortable.

"Yes?"

"I have been watching you very closely. I have seen you develop from someone with mere talent to a disciplined, skilled craftsman."

Bezalel shifted uneasily. He had no idea where this was going.

"I've also seen that your God possesses powerful magic," Khafra went on. "I have a request of you. Marry my daughter, Karem. Become my son. My own son has no interest or skill in our craft. When I am old, I will need someone to take over from me. I will make you overseer in my stead. I would like someone with your skill, wisdom, and power in charge of the shop."

He stopped and looked at Bezalel as if waiting for answer.

Bezalel stared at the ground, silent. He had never expected this. Just weeks ago, such an offer would have made him ecstatic. Moses' coming had changed all that.

But he couldn't just say no to Khafra. Though his overseer was usually a patient, even stoic man, he also had pride and a temper, which Bezalel didn't want to rouse.

"I… I don't know…"

Khafra's eyes lit up as they probed Bezalel's face. "You don't have to thank me," he said. "And excuse Karem's outburst today. She'll get over being upset about the gardens. She'll be pleased to know we have spoken. She has always admired and thought highly of you."

CHAPTER

eight

THE WORLD LOOKED LIKE A SKELETON OF ITSELF. NOT A LEAF, BLOSSOM, or blade of grass remained. A wind had come up in the night and blown away the insects that had tormented them for days. The stillness after days of chirping, jumping locusts made Pi-Ramesses seem like an even more desolate place.

The devastation Bezalel saw as he walked from the slave encampment to the shop seemed a reflection of his own situation. Why had he been silent and not voiced his feelings to Khafra? Anything would be better than being trapped in Egypt while his people went free. He had to find an opportunity to let Khafra know that marrying Karem and becoming his son-in-law and heir was something he could never do.

Bezalel's chairs were almost done. As Khafra watched him gild the carved arms and legs, a smile played behind his eyes and around his mouth. He observed for a while, left, and returned shortly to stand over Bezalel as he worked.

"Nicely done," he said. "Pharaoh will be pleased, and even more when he finds that you will someday be the head of his goldsmiths. Come with me now. We must talk."

He led Bezalel to a side room of the shop, away from the curious eyes and ears of the others. There was a man there with a razor, a kilt, and a linen robe of the type Khafra himself wore.

"Now that you will soon be my son, we must make you look like one of us," said Khafra. He turned to the waiting man. "Shave his hair and his beard."

Bezalel, seeing what was about to happen, took a step backward toward the door. "Sir," he said, "I cannot do this. My family doesn't know. I would want their blessing. I need some time, please. Let me continue as I am for now."

The expression on Khafra's face changed from surprise to annoyance. "Do you not realize what an honor I'm bestowing on you?" he asked. "How can the approval of your family matter? They are mere slaves. Come now, be reasonable."

Bezalel put his hands to his head as if to protect his hair from the razor. "No! I can't do this," he said, desperation in his voice.

"What do you mean, 'can't do this'?" There was a cold edge to Khafra's voice. "It's all arranged."

More of Khafra's servants must have been in the room, for now rough hands grabbed Bezalel from behind and pushed him toward the man with the razor. Terror rose in him. He had never been a fighter. He was no match for the strength he felt in the steel fingers that gripped both arms. Maybe if he didn't resist, they would loosen. He willed himself to go limp and felt the hold on him relax ever so slightly.

"Bring him here," Khafra said, his voice quiet and hard. "He will be one of us."

"No!" Bezalel shouted. With all his might, he twisted out of his captor's grip, broke free, and ran through the shop out into the street.

"Catch him!" he heard behind him.

He ran past the workers' encampment and through the market, not daring to look back. Panting, he ducked to catch his breath between the stall of a man selling geese and another selling fish. But a minute later, three of Khafra's servants bounded into view.

Slipping behind the market stalls, he jogged through streets lined with houses. He had never been here before but was sure he was near the canal. Once he found it, he knew the way to Goshen.

At last the canal came into sight. The bank beside the water was steep but grassy. He eased himself partway down the embankment, pressed himself into the grass, and waited for sunset.

Hours later, he set out again and had nearly reached the city gates when he heard footsteps. His backward glance revealed two figures, gaining on him at every step. He quickened his pace, but a minute later one and then the other grabbed him.

* * *

When Bezalel woke the next morning, it was still dark. He eased into a different position, favoring his back. It was sore from the beating he had received on his return. He was trapped in the city. Would his family leave Egypt without him? He lay wide awake on his mat for what seemed like a long time, wondering when morning would come.

He heard stirring next to him, where Shoshan slept.

"How are you feeling?" Shoshan asked. He had rubbed oil on Bezalel's welts when he'd been brought back to the encampment after Khafra administered his punishment.

"I'm okay," said Bezalel. "But I'm wide awake."

He got up and made his way to the entrance. He couldn't see a thing. Not even the two guards who had stationed themselves there last night were visible. In the sky was no sign of the thinning darkness of dawn.

"It certainly is black out there," he said on his return to the sleeping quarters. "But it's a strange darkness, heavy and blacker than black."

The men groped for their clothes and got dressed. Someone lit a torch but the flame died almost immediately, as if a hand had snuffed it out. In the blackness, Bezalel listened. He heard a crying baby, a barking dog, and off in the distance a keening wail. That would be the priests pleading with Ra, the sun god, to appear, for by now, judging from the hollowness in his stomach, the usual time of daybreak was long past.

The day dragged. It was too dark to find one's way outside, so the men stayed in the encampment. Bezalel told them of his attempt to go back to Goshen the previous day and of his last visit home, when he had met Moses.

"He said the people should get ready to leave Goshen," Bezalel said. "I only hope my family hasn't left without me."

"Do you really think Pharaoh will let us go?" Shoshan asked.

"If it were only up to him, no," Bezalel said. "But the more I see, the more I realize that Yahweh has power. What else could this darkness mean?"

"Do you think it's another sign?" asked one of the other Hebrews.

"I do," said Bezalel. "Who do the Egyptians worship as their highest god? The sun god Ra. This darkness shows them that even powerful Ra can't stand in the face of Yahweh's wishes. I heard Moses say that all these signs are meant to help the Egyptians, and us Hebrews, learn about Yahweh's power firsthand."

"I wish He'd show His power now and make it get light," said Shoshan.

"So do I," said Bezalel. "First chance I get, I'm leaving here."

"We're with you," said Shoshan and the others.

CHAPTER
nine

AS THE DARKNESS CONTINUED INTO THE NEXT DAY, BEZALEL FOUGHT overwhelming uneasiness. The increasing volume and desperation in the chants and prayers of Pharaoh's priests fed his fears.

Terrible thoughts prowled his mind. What if the sun never came out again? What if Yahweh wasn't behind this and the reason Egypt was in the dark was because Ra was angry? No, he told himself. That could never be. This must be another sign from Yahweh.

Again he took a long hard look at what he actually believed. He couldn't remember exactly when he had turned his back on the God of his mother's stories. It had been a gradual switch of loyalties, he supposed. Watching how his family prayed but nothing happened. Working on the Egyptian images with their magic powers. Being told over and over that his talent was a blessing of the gods. Identifying with Ptah as his inspiration and protector.

But the last months had changed all that. Yahweh was real. He did have power. He had seen it with his own eyes. Now that Yahweh was about to free the Israelites and his family from Egyptian slavery, Bezalel had to go with them.

Still, he was also a part of Egypt, and Egypt was a part of him. The amulet around his neck reminded him of that connection. He had a sense that if he really wanted to be on Yahweh's side, he would need to remove the charm.

But wasn't that dangerous? What if he took it off only to find that Yahweh's power wasn't supreme? Would angering Ptah rob him of his skill?

Then again, maybe his talents had nothing to do with Ptah or any Egyptian god. He'd had skill in his hands for as long as he could remember. Maybe it was the way *Yahweh* had made him.

He thought back and realized that this fight for his loyalty had been going on for weeks. As it raged now in the oppressive darkness, he knew it was time to make a decision. Did he dare remove the amulet? Was he ready?

In his mind, he formed words of his own to the God of his people. "Yahweh, You are all-powerful. I want to be on Your side, loyal to You. Please bring the light again and help me get home to my family." Then, grasping and pulling with both hands, he broke the chain that held the charm around his neck. The gold pendant clattered heavily onto the ground.

Even as he prayed, he sensed that Yahweh saw him and looked kindly on him. In place of his fear was a carefree lightness. Inside, he felt like a bird released from its cage.

* * *

The darkness lasted for another day. By the end of the third, the slaves had eaten all the food stashed in the encampment and were nearly out of water, so when the sun rose for the first time in four days, a cheer went up from everyone in the workers' hovel and throughout the city.

In the hours of darkness, Bezalel had mulled over how he could escape. At first light, he ran to the entrance of the encampment and saw that the men who had stood guard were gone. Now was the time. Only, he couldn't go without his tools. Did he dare risk going to the shop to collect them?

"The guards are gone," he told Shoshan as he gathered his possessions and tied them in a bundle. "I'm going to get my tools and leave for Goshen."

"I'm with you," said Shoshan.

The two of them ran with their bundles into the still-dim morning. They weren't the only ones about, for the shop was already open, though their cautious entry revealed no one there.

Bezalel saw that someone had gathered his tools from where he had left them four days ago. He went to where they were stored, collected them, and was just tying them into an old robe when he sensed someone watching him. He looked up to see the Egyptian who was responsible for opening the shop.

"What are you doing?" the Egyptian asked.

Before thinking about the impact of his words he said, "I'm gathering my tools and leaving for Goshen."

Their eyes locked for a long moment. Then the Egyptian said simply, "Go."

With that, Bezalel and Shoshan hoisted their bundles onto their backs and hurried into the brightening morning.

PART TWO

Free

CHAPTER
ten

GOSHEN HAD CHANGED SINCE BEZALEL HAD LAST BEEN HOME. ITS pathways were abuzz with comings and goings. There were shouts of welcome and hugs as people returned home from places of slavery. Many were sitting outside their homes making tents and weaving baskets in preparation for leaving. Foreigners were there too, setting up makeshift dwellings among the people.

At home, Bezalel received an enthusiastic welcome.

"Welcome home, son!" Grandpa Hur engulfed Bezalel in a hug and nearly squeezed the breath out of him. "Where's your idol?"

"I took it off," Bezalel said, giving his grandfather a sheepish grin.

A smile lit the old man's face. "Praise Yahweh!"

As he told them about Khafra's offer and his foiled attempt to return home a few days earlier, Noemi shook her head in disbelief. "We were so close to losing you," she said, putting her warm, work-worn hands over his.

"I'm so glad you're still here," said Bezalel. "I was afraid I'd be left behind."

* * *

"Moses has made changes in the calendar," Hur told Bezalel that evening at supper. "He has renamed this the month of Nisan. Special things are to happen. Each family is to select a perfect yearling lamb, sheep, or goat and slaughter it on the fourteenth day of the month."

"It sounds complicated," said Bezalel.

"If only that were all," said Hur. "Moses has asked me to help spread the word to the families of our tribe. Would you like to help?"

And so the next few days found Bezalel going around, spreading the instructions for the Lord's Passover to the families of Judah. It was a meal the people were to eat after slaughtering the chosen lamb and painting its drained blood on the sides and tops of the doorframes of their houses. Bezalel wasn't sure why the directions were so detailed or particular, but he made certain to pass them along precisely as Hur had told him: "Eat the meat roasted over the fire along with bitter herbs and unleavened bread. Do not eat the meat raw or cooked in water but roasted over the fire, head, legs and inner parts. Do not leave any of it until morning. If some is left, you must burn it. This is how you are to eat it: with your cloak tucked into your belt, your sandals on your feet, and your staff in your hand. Eat it in haste. It is the Lord's Passover."

These final instructions especially fired Bezalel's imagination. They sounded like the beginning of an adventure!

* * *

"Do you know what this is about?" asked one of the men who had worked under Uri.

"Something to do with the new celebration we're to hold tomorrow, I think," said Uri. "Maybe instructions for leaving."

"Do you really think we'll actually be allowed to go?" someone else asked.

It was the day before the new celebration. Moses and Aaron had called a meeting of the people. Messengers sent from the elders of each tribe spread the word around Goshen: "It's imperative that household elders attend."

Bezalel had accompanied his father and grandfather. The public square was teeming with people. The atmosphere was one of excitement. When Moses and Aaron arrived, a hush fell over the crowd. In their usual back-and-forth way, Moses spoke quietly to Aaron, and Aaron broadcast to the people what Moses had said.

"Tomorrow is a momentous day. You will remember it forever. In fact, the feast you celebrate for the first time tomorrow, you are to celebrate every year from now on. Listen closely. It's very important that you follow these instructions to the last detail.

"When you go home tonight, or at the very latest tomorrow morning, slaughter the animal you have chosen. Catch its blood in a basin. Then take a branch of hyssop and paint its blood on the top and both sides of the doorframe.

"After sunset tomorrow, do not go out of the door of your house until morning. Tomorrow night the Lord will go through the land to strike the Egyptians. When He sees the blood on the top and sides of the doorframe, He will pass over that doorway and not permit the destroyer to enter your house and strike down your firstborn, as He will strike the Egyptians.

"After Yahweh has struck the Egyptians, they will be eager for you to go. Then you are to ask them for anything of value—clothing for your children, gold and silver armbands, bracelets, earrings, fingerings, collars. They will give you anything you desire. So you shall plunder the Egyptians.

"And when you leave, arrange yourselves in orderly ranks so no one is trampled and everyone accounted for. In the meantime, prepare the meal as you were instructed. Roast the meat. Season it with bitter herbs. Prepare unleavened bread."

Moses was finished. Discussion buzzed all around. Some called out questions:

"When will we be leaving?"

"What if we forget and go outside by mistake?"

"I heard from someone that we are to burn the leftovers from the meal…"

Aaron began to answer, "About the time of leaving…"

Moses cut in: "You have heard what I said and the instructions I gave. Now go home and follow them. Your leaving will unfold as Yahweh wills."

* * *

Uri, Hur, and Bezalel went home to a dilemma. Which would be their chosen lamb? Of the six yearlings they possessed, only Zamri's pet Curls had no blemish.

"I know it will break her heart if we take her lamb," Uri said, "but all the others are obviously flawed. We cannot celebrate this feast for the very first time with an imperfect animal."

"Let me talk to her," said Hur.

Zamri was helping Noemi with washing clothes. They had just returned from the river with baskets loaded with wet laundry and were hanging the garments near the house wherever there was air movement to dry them.

"Zamri, I need to talk to you," said Hur.

"Sure, Grandpa," she said, dropping the tunic she was holding, skipping over to him, and taking his hand. Though she was already fourteen and almost old enough to marry, to Bezalel she still seemed like the little girl he had spoiled and protected before he was sent off to work in Pi-Ramesses.

"Let's go for a walk," Hur said.

Bezalel shuddered to think how Hur's request would affect his sister. He reached for the garment Zamri had dropped and took up the job of helping his mother hang the clothes.

"Do you know what your father wants?" asked Noemi.

"It has something to do with Curls," replied Uri.

"Oh yes, that matter," said Noemi. "We might be in for a tearful afternoon."

Hur and Zamri came back about half an hour later. Zamri's eyes were red and puffy, her manner subdued. But she also looked resolute as she went over to Uri. "Daddy, you can have Curls," she said. "I don't want Bezalel to die."

A shiver went through Bezalel. But yes, this Passover, with its need for a perfect lamb and its blood painted on the doorposts, did affect him as the firstborn son. Suddenly, the whole thing didn't seem like quite such an adventure. There would be a price to pay. It was already being exacted.

CHAPTER
eleven

BEZALEL WOKE THE NEXT MORNING TO THE SMELL OF BAKING BREAD. His mother must have risen very early to make the dough and ready the fire. He lay awake, replaying scenes from yesterday—his father taking Curls away from their house (Uri did the deed while Bezalel hugged Zamri, who sobbed into his shoulder), his grandfather painting the blood around the doorway, Noemi washing the parsley, peeling and chopping the horseradish amidst tears as the odor from the bitter root filled the air.

He looked around the small room where he had slept all his life. The walls, on which formerly had hung papyrus drawings from when he was a youngster, were bare. All his possessions were bundled and tied. He got up, went to the old robe that held his tools, and untied it. The worn fabric cradled the objects that had been his companions for the last nine years—the crucible, tongs, bellows, and beeswax for casting. The smoothing stone, mallet, knife, bradawl, and a couple of chisels for overlaying and carving. The sight of them comforted him. As long as he had these tools, he was still himself—the wielder of carving and gold-working magic. He wrapped them again, tied them tightly so none would work its way out, and left the parcel beside his other possessions.

He stepped into the main room of the house and saw that it was in chaos.

"Bezalel, I need your help," his mother said as she caught sight of him. Her pursed forehead told him she was tense. "Could you gather the clothes from outside? Then look through these clothes for ones strong enough to wrap our pots. Go to the storage room and gather baskets. Also, we need to fill these jugs with water…" When there were preparations to be made, his mother became an Egyptian taskmaster.

The day, which Bezalel had feared would drag by, flew as he helped first his mother with her multitude of tasks, then his father and grandfather by stitching pieces of hide into a tent. By the time the late afternoon sun slipped through the windows, the house smelled of herbs and roast lamb. And then, as Zamri finished laying the last of the dishes on the table, Uri closed the door against a blood-red sky. The night of Passover had begun. They would eat the meal and see what happened next.

On this special night, Hur began the meal by reciting the blessing. "The Lord will provide. Blessing I will bless you, and multiplying I will multiply your descendants as the stars of the heaven and as the sand which is on the seashore. And your descendants shall possess the gate of their enemies. In your seed all the nations of the earth shall be blessed. The words of Yahweh to our father Abraham."

Though Bezalel had listened to Hur recite these words many times, for the first time in his life he actually heard them and they thrilled him. As someone who had returned to Yahweh from the gods of the Egyptians, they were now for him too.

The meal, though simple, was delicious. Noemi had added to the menu celery, parsley, and boiled eggs, and for the meat Charoset—a paste of chopped nuts, dates, spice, and sweet red wine. The only sad person was Zamri. She couldn't bear to eat the lamb and Uri had to get very firm with her before she would eat anything at all.

As usual, Noemi had made too much food. When they had all eaten their fill, there was a large portion of meat left over. "We'll leave it for a few hours," said Uri, "in case someone gets hungry and wants to pick at it. Otherwise we must burn it."

That brought another burst of tears from Zamri.

After the meal, the family sat around the table talking. The early morning and long day of preparation seemed to have exhausted Noemi, for she kept nodding off to sleep.

"Here, I'll spread out the bedroll and you can nap," said Uri.

Noemi lay down in her clothes and was soon breathing deeply and evenly. About an hour later, Zamri joined her.

But Uri, Hur, and Bezalel sat around the table and talked. Hur told stories of the time when he and Aaron were young, and how Pharaoh's daughter had found the baby Moses and raised him in the palace.

Bezalel had heard the story before, but he loved hearing it again. "What was Moses like as a boy?" he asked.

"We didn't see him much until he was older," said Hur. "Thirty-eight. Thirty-nine. He started visiting Goshen then. Got to know Miriam and Aaron. He was very intense and serious. You may have noticed the same thing in him now when…"

A faint wail sounded in the distance. Hur stopped talking and they all listened. There it was again, only louder.

Bezalel got up and went toward the door, but Uri jumped up and blocked his way.

"No," he said. "We're not to go out."

The three men listened, as the wailing grew louder, nearer, and soon surrounded them. Then there was a pounding at the door. Uri opened it to find his Egyptian overseer and a woman Bezalel assumed was his wife.

"Go," said the man, without uttering any of the formalities of greeting.

"What will convince you to leave?" asked the wild-eyed woman at his side. She thrust a handful of jewelry at Uri. "Take these and go."

"Why? What has happened?" asked Uri. He looked stunned.

"Our son, Thutmos. Dead. We told Pharaoh to let you leave long ago, but he wouldn't listen. Now this." The woman covered her face and keened into her hands.

Bezalel thought of Khafra and wondered, had this night of death killed his son? He shook his head as he thought of how that would devastate his overseer.

The commotion woke Noemi and Zamri, and they rose.

"I'm so sorry," said Noemi, walking toward the woman as if to console her.

"Don't touch me!" the woman shrieked. "Stay away from me, you woman of magic. Just leave Egypt." She loosened a rich-looking gold collar from around her neck and took off her linen overdress. "If I give you these, will you go?" She flung the clothes and adornments at Noemi.

The couple left but was followed by other Egyptians the family had known, each with the same tale of death, each begging the Israelites to go. Noemi followed Moses' instructions and asked for gold and garments to take with them. So eager were the Egyptians to see them leave that they came and went throughout the night with linen robes, kilts, tunics, and all manner of jewelry. The first rays of the sun shone through the windows a few hours later on a sizeable pile of garments and a glittering heap of gold, silver, and jeweled trinkets that had grown steadily in the last hours of the night.

twelve CHAPTER

THE FIRST HOURS OF DAYLIGHT SAW GOSHEN ERUPT IN A BEDLAM OF activity. Egyptians kept coming as they had through the night, bringing with them anything of value to induce the Israelites to leave, and leave now.

Bezalel's family burned the last of the Passover meal, then gathered their possessions. Each person was laden with bundles. Noemi wrapped some of the Egyptian clothing from last night around the kneading trough, heavy with unleavened bread dough, and Uri carried it on his back. Bezalel's bundle contained some of last night's plunder as well as his tools, a few extra clothes, and a canteen of water.

They tied baskets of flour, oil, salt, the last of the bread, and the remains of the garden to the sides of their goat. They roped their small herd of animals together and as a family joined the river of people marching away from Goshen toward the desert.

There was an air of ecstasy throughout the crowd. Groups sang. Friends and family members talked and laughed, recounting their experiences of the last hours. Children dashed around the legs of adults and animals, playing games of tag and hide-and-seek. Even the heat, which soon became oppressive, didn't seem to bother most people.

Bezalel, unaccustomed to spending long hours under the hot sun, soon got a headache. When the family stopped for a break, he took a long drink of water. Then Noemi soaked a cloth and had him tie it around his head.

They walked, and walked, and walked until finally someone up ahead called a halt.

"Where are we?" Bezalel asked.

Uri and Hur weren't sure, but nearby someone who had been this way before said he thought it was a place called Succoth.

Uri and Bezalel scouted a level spot for the tent and put it up. Nearby they found a scrubby tree to which they tied their animals. Noemi sent Zamri to collect rocks to make a fire pit. The comforting smell of bread sharpened Bezalel's appetites. The meal was meager compared to the feast they'd had the night before, but to hungry Bezalel it was just as satisfying.

The day wasn't over, however, for as they finished the meal, a messenger came with orders that they were to gather on a nearby hillside for a message from Moses.

Noemi and Zamri did a quick cleanup, then the family joined the crowds thronging toward the meeting spot. They soon came to a hillside in an amphitheater shape where people already sat on the circle of hillocks that sloped toward the valley. Moses and Aaron stood at the bottom, waiting for the people to arrive.

Bezalel and his family found a spot on the prickly grass and sat down as people continued to assemble.

Bezalel scanned the crowds. There were so many. Hundreds of thousands. How had they all made it this far? How would Moses get such a multitude to… exactly where? He had no concept of where Canaan was.

His thoughts were interrupted as Moses, then Aaron, began speaking in their customary back-and-forth manner.

"This has been quite a day. Today, in this month of Nisan, you are leaving the land of Egypt. Remember this day. Celebrate it because the Lord brought you out of Egypt with a mighty hand."

Moses smiled as he said these words. Bezalel had never seen him smile before.

"When the Lord brings you into the land of the Canaanites, Hittites, Amorites, Hivites, and Jebusites, the land He swore to your forefathers to give to you, a land flowing with milk and honey, you are to observe this ceremony in this month."

Moses and Aaron went on to explain how the Israelites were to take all yeast from their homes and eat only unleavened bread on this feast day. Furthermore, they were to give God the first male offspring of each member of their herd of livestock. Even the firstborn donkey required the sacrifice of a lamb.

"This observance will be for you like a sign on your hand and a reminder on your forehead that the law of the Lord is to be on your lips," Moses said. "In this way you are to redeem your firstborn sons."

As Moses mentioned firstborn sons, Zamri, who was sitting next to him, snuggled close. A wave of affection for his little sister washed over Bezalel and he put his arm around her, giving her a squeeze. Only now did he realize how much he had missed her and his whole family.

Moses was still talking. Bezalel switched his attention back to the speech.

"In the days ahead, when your son asks why you are doing this, tell him, 'I do this because of what the Lord did for me when I came out of Egypt. He brought me with a mighty hand out of slavery while He killed every firstborn son and animal in Egypt. So celebrate this day.

Let it be a sign on your hand and a symbol on your forehead that it was Yahweh who brought you out of Egypt with His mighty hand.'"

Moses' speech was ended. The crowds began leaving, chattering as they went.

Bezalel's legs ached as he stood up with the others. But despite his weariness, he wondered if his excitement at finally seeing this day would even let him sleep.

* * *

The next morning, Bezalel woke to find that only he and Zamri still slept. He pulled on his clothes in a hurry. It was cold in the tent. The air here at the edge of the desert was different from hot, humid Egypt—cold at night, though it had been unbearably hot during the day.

He went outside to find his mother preparing food. Father and Hur tended to the animals.

"Get Zamri up, please," said Noemi. "We have to pack the tent and be ready to move out shortly."

Bezalel reentered the stuffy skin shelter. "Zamri, time to get up," he said, shaking her by the shoulder.

"Go away." She turned over to face the other direction.

"Zamri, get up. Father wants to take the tent down."

"Ooooh." She groaned and sat up. Bezalel left to let her get dressed.

"Go fill this jug," Noemi told him now, handing him the water jug that had been full when they'd left Goshen yesterday. "Someone said there is a well down there somewhere." She pointed in the direction of a grove of palms a short walk away.

Bezalel took the jug and joined dozens of others with their jugs and leather flasks.

As he walked, he overheard the conversation two men ahead of him were having. "Where exactly are we headed?" asked one.

"I assume it's Canaan, where Abraham, Isaac, and Jacob are buried," said the other. "It should be at most a journey of several weeks."

"Have you traveled that road?"

"No. But some of the men on my work crew know it well. They called it the Way of the Philistines. It follows the Great Sea, like this." He stooped down and drew a picture in the sand. "Here is Goshen and the Great Sea. And here is Succoth, where we are now. As we continue north, we will get to that road. It crosses the Wilderness of Zin to the land of our fathers."

"Are there wells and oases and such along it?"

"Oh yes. But fierce tribes too. Nomads that might give us trouble."

Bezalel didn't catch any more of the conversation when the crowds of water-seekers thickened and other jug-carriers came between him and the conversants. Bezalel spent a long time in line waiting for his turn at the well. As they inched along, impatient thoughts threatened to darken the sunny morning. Is this what their new life would be made of—walking and waiting, then walking and waiting some more? This was only the beginning. He'd better get used to walking and waiting.

When he got back with the water, the family was ready to leave. Already the sun was high and burned his head. Before setting off, he wet a cloth and put it on top of his head as he had the day before.

The day was as strenuous as yesterday had been. Bezalel noticed a change in the mood of the travelers. People walked along in silence. It seemed they had exhausted their excitement. Children whined that they were tired, that they wanted a drink. Where were they going, they asked, and when would they get there? Mothers replied in a variety of patient, weary, and sharp tones.

Ahead, Bezalel caught sight of a familiar shape. Shoshan!

"I've got to talk to my friend," he said to his family. He forged through the ranks to his fellow worker. "Shoshan!" he called as he caught up with his friend and pounded him on the back.

"Bezalel!"

The two embraced.

"Did the others make it?" asked Bezalel.

"Yes. They left the same day we did. I talked to Benjamin. He said Khafra was beside himself with anger when he found we had sneaked away."

Talking with Shoshan helped the hours of walking pass quickly, so that Bezalel was surprised when they stopped.

"I'd better get back to my family," he said, "or we'll lose each other for good in these crowds."

The place where they stopped was called Etham, he discovered. It was a small settlement on the edge of the desert.

Several times during the day, Bezalel noted a cloud in the sky. He had expected it to drift overhead, maybe even relieve the heat with a shower. But it stayed just ahead of them all day.

After supper, he sat with his family around the fire. They watched the sun set, but he noticed that the cloud was still there. In fact, it had changed from puffy white to a glowing presence, rivaling the moon in brightness.

"Look at that cloud," said Zamri. "What is it?"

"I have a feeling about it," said Hur. "Perhaps Yahweh hasn't left all His signs in Egypt."

thirteen CHAPTER

"I THINK WE'VE TAKEN A WRONG TURN," SAID SOMEONE WALKING NEAR Bezalel.

"I can tell by the sun that we're heading southeast," said another. "The way to the shortest road to Canaan is north."

"I wonder about that Moses," said still another.

The complaints of those around him planted a seed of worry in Bezalel. It was the seventh day out of Egypt. They hadn't made much progress in those days, and now a wrong turn? Bezalel too realized they had changed direction from the one described by the man who had drawn their route on the ground. Did Moses really know the way?

As the day wore on, Bezalel kept an eye on yesterday's cloud, which was still in the sky. People speculated about what it meant. Some said they were familiar with desert travel and had seen such a phenomenon before. Others said it was nothing, a mere coincidence of nature. Someone else said he had heard Moses say the cloud was Yahweh's presence leading them. Bezalel hoped it was the last.

Their endless course led through a changing landscape. Late in the day the hills on either side of the path became tall and steep. Off in the distance were the palms of a wadi. Someone said it was Migdol, but they passed it and continued walking. Finally the path narrowed, with cliffs on either side. Word drifted back from those ahead. They had come to Pa Hahiroth.

The forward momentum of the crowd slowed as their route squeezed between high, steep rocks. At last Bezalel and his family got through the narrow section and saw a large area where people sere setting up tents. Except for that level section, they were surrounded by mountains. And on the side with no mountains, there was water. How would they get anywhere from here without retracing their steps?

The small camping space meant neighbors had to crowd in close. Bezalel's family set up their tent and settled in faster than ever before. Practice was making them efficient as each did his or her job in record time. Noemi had just set a pot of water on the fire when someone ran by with an unbelievable message: "The Egyptians are coming!"

"What did he say?" asked Hur. His hearing wasn't as sharp as it had once been.

"He said the Egyptians are coming," said Uri, "though he must be wrong. Winds kick up the dust all the time out here. It's probably just a sandstorm."

But a few minutes later, a couple of terrified men ran down the path. Uri stopped them. "What is it?" he asked.

"We were on the cliffs, looking behind us. We saw the Egyptians," said one of the men, so out of breath he could hardly get the words out.

"We saw clouds in the distance. As they got closer, we made out horses and chariots. They're coming this way! I must find Moses and tell him." With that, the man ran on.

Word of the Egyptian chariots spread through the camp like a grass fire. The woman in the next tent clung to two little children and began wailing as she rocked them back and forth. The air was filled with frightened and angry words.

"What has Moses done, bringing us out of Egypt?"

"Didn't we tell him to leave us alone and let us just carry on being slaves?"

"It would have been better to stay where we were than die out here at the point of Egyptian swords!"

Bezalel's heart pounded as panic engulfed him. How could things have gone so terribly wrong? This felt like a bad dream. Would he have to go back and face Khafra again? After the beating he had received, returning to the shop was unimaginable.

The cries all around augmented his own fear and he knew he had to get away. Maybe there was a road out of this valley that one couldn't see from here. He would go look for himself.

Winding his way through the Israelite camp, he only saw more of the same. People were weeping and shouting at each other in panic. Men were clustered in heated conversation. Some raised fists toward the front of the multitude and uttered oaths as if threatening their leader.

Finally, Bezalel came to the last of the crowd, stopped by a low cliff that looked over the sea. And there was Moses.

He lay facedown on the ground, obviously praying, the tone of his voice pleading and desperate. This didn't bode well. But even as Bezalel studied him, he rose.

Bezalel scanned his face as he stood. His eyes looked as penetrating as ever and there was in them not a hint of the emotion Bezalel had just heard in his voice. Instead there was determination in his jaw and decisiveness in his words.

"God has spoken to me," he said to Aaron, who stood beside him. "Tell the people to prepare to leave."

Aaron, who had by now engaged a group of young men to act as messengers, gathered them around and gave instructions. "Tell the people Moses says you are to pack up. Get ready to move on."

Bezalel was aghast. He looked around at the water in front of them and the towering cliffs. They couldn't go through the sea and surely Moses wasn't going to lead them through the mountains.

He watched as Moses walked toward the water. At the cliff edge, he raised his staff over the sea and held it high. This was the rod that had changed into a snake. What would it do now? Bezalel kept his eyes on it but it held its shape.

No rafts or boats appeared in the water that crashed into the driftwood-littered beach below, but a wind began to blow even as Moses held his rod steady. Bezalel sensed something momentous was about to happen. He'd better get back to his family.

As he retraced his steps, he saw the people were indeed packing up, though the complaining hadn't abated.

"What are we doing?"

"Where is there a way out of this mess? We're trapped!"

"Slavery was better than this confusion."

Back with his family, Uri and Hur had taken down the tent.

"Where were you?" Noemi asked him.

"I saw Moses," Bezalel replied. "He's holding his rod over the sea. Something strange is about to happen."

"I hope so," said Uri. "If we stay much longer, the Egyptians will be upon us."

Bezalel looked in the direction that the Egyptians were advancing, but the cliffs lining the entryway to their camp area were now obscured.

"Look at the cloud," Bezalel exclaimed. "It has come between us and the Egyptians."

"I see the hand of God in this," said Hur.

Messengers spreading Moses' instructions interrupted them. "Moses says to you, 'Do not be afraid. Stand firm and you will see the deliverance the Lord will bring you. The Egyptians you see today you will never see again. The Lord will fight for you; you need only be still.'"

The man had to shout to be heard above the wind, which whipped his words away from their ears.

"Yahweh be praised!" said Hur.

"What did you say?" asked Noemi.

"The sand is hurting my skin and stinging my eyes," Zamri said.

"Cover your face with your robe," Bezalel said, showing her how to wrap herself in the fabric of her outer garment to protect her face and arms from the grit that now filled the air.

"Pick up your stuff," said Uri. "Make sure we have everything. We're moving!"

CHAPTER

fourteen

BEZALEL'S FAMILY TOOK THEIR PLACES AS THE CROWD SURGED TOWARD the water. What would they find when they got there, Bezalel wondered, thinking of the waves he had seen crashing against the beach a short while before.

Surprisingly they continued to advance. Bezalel, who knew their family was somewhere in the middle of the multitude, wondered how they could keep going. The water wasn't that far away. Surely the front of the crowd had already been stopped by it.

Then he noticed that the ground beneath his feet was firm, smooth and damp, as if there had been rain. Looking to either side, he noticed not rock but water—walls of water. Even in the gathering darkness, he could tell what it was.

"Are we walking right through the seabed?" he shouted to his father.

"What did you say?" Uri cupped his hand over his ear.

Bezalel repeated his question, shouting right into Uri's ear. "We're walking through the sea."

"I think you're right," said Uri. A smile of relief lit up his face. "God has sent a wind to make a path through the sea for us."

And then they were on dry ground again. Judging by the rubble that littered the surface, they had reached the opposite shore. They moved on until they were well away from the seabed.

All around them people were buzzing in amazement. "We walked right through the sea. We're on the other side. We made it!"

Bezalel helped his father put up the tent. But though by now it was dark and he had walked many hours, he didn't want to sleep.

"I'm going to the beach to watch," he said.

"I want to come with you," Zamri said.

Noemi seemed to hesitate. "You'll look out for her?" she asked Bezalel.

"Of course."

The terrain on this side of the water wasn't as steep. Zamri and he found a spot on a hillside overlooking the scene. From this vantage point, they took in the amazing sight, for water had indeed piled up and formed a wall on both sides of a path. The Israelites walked down that path. The crowd still stretched to the other side, silhouetted against the glowing cloud, which rested behind them obscuring the cliffs and the Egyptian army.

They watched for what seemed like an hour or more. Bezalel felt Zamri's body lean against his and her head sag onto his shoulder. He laid her back, putting her cloak behind her head to protect it from the ground and covering her with the rest of it. He lay back beside her.

Sometime later, he awoke with a start. He sat up. It was light. All around, the hillside was crowded with people. Someone's shout of "No!" had woken him. He looked ahead to where last night, in the light of the moon and luminous cloud, the people had crossed. Now Egyptian chariots were careening through the place where they had camped. He watched, horrified, as the lead chariots raced onto the seabed.

Zamri sat up and rubbed her eyes. "Where am I?"

"We're beside the Red Sea. Remember how we crossed last night?"

"What's happening?" Zamri asked, becoming aware of drama playing out in front of them. "Are those Egyptians? Oh no! They're still coming after us!"

The dismay in her voice was echoed all around them as people watched the Egyptians advance along the same path that had opened through the water for the Israelites. Like animals paralyzed by the advance of a deadly snake, they stared in open-mouthed horror at the approaching chariots and horses.

But wait. Bezalel saw that something was hindering their progress. The horses had started sinking into the mud. The closer they got to the center, the deeper they sank until they were up to their knees and hocks in the mud, then lunging to get free. With each lunge, they sank even deeper.

Panicked drivers whipped the frantic animals. This only caused more jumping, writhing, sinking. A wheel came off one of the chariots. Slowly the vehicle lost balance and tipped over, throwing its driver out and under the hooves of a crazed horse. More chariots overturned as drivers tried without success to turn them around and retreat onto dry ground.

Bezalel and Zamri joined the other onlookers in a great cheer as water from both walls began trickling down and then gushing to fill the seabed and float the wheels, pieces of wood, and broken-up chariots. The horses that were still alive swam past, their eyes full of terror. Others, with rumps in the air, floated by or washed up on the opposite shore to join the shoreline debris of armor and men. By mid-morning, there was no sign of the path through the sea, though the water was still littered with bodies and broken chariots.

Bezalel and Zamri found their way back to their family's tent. What a change in the feeling of the camp, Bezalel thought, remembering the terror, fear, and panic of only hours before. It was as if the sun had appeared from behind a thundercloud—no, had evaporated the thundercloud. As the two passed through the camp, the people's voices around them rang with joy, laughter, and singing.

News of the Egyptians' destruction had already reached Noemi, Uri, and Hur. They listened with delight and amazement as Bezalel and Zamri described what they had seen at night and then recounted the Egyptians' final defeat.

"Praise Yahweh! He has destroyed the Egyptians so they can never hurt us again," Hur said.

After they had eaten, Uri wanted to go to the beach to see the battle-front for himself. Bezalel took him to the place he and Zamri had spent the night. The shorelines on both sides were now littered with bodies and carcasses, along with bits of harness, whips, the ripped webbing of chariot floors, wheels, and wood.

"Just think, we walked through that seabed just last night with the Egyptians on our heels," said Uri in awe. "And now we find ourselves here with not one life lost, not even an animal missing. Moses was right when he said the Lord would fight for us. What a miracle!"

They walked back toward their tent through a party-like atmosphere. All around, the people had taken out instruments and were celebrating with lyres, flutes, cymbals, and timbrels. Others sang and danced. The men passed Moses' and Aaron's tents and there was Moses, singing as loudly as any of them.

"I will sing to the Lord
For He is highly exalted
The horse and its rider
He has hurled into the sea."

Uri and Bezalel stopped to join the growing crowd around Moses. How strange, yet wonderful, to see that their intense, serious leader knew how to celebrate too.

When Moses finished his song, he sang it again and onlookers joined in. With rare spontaneity, he began moving through the crowds. Soon a line of singers and dancers formed behind him. The line of men wove its way singing, clapping, and dancing through the camp. Bezalel and Uri fell into step. Along the way, they passed the family's camp, where Hur joined them.

Moses led them back to his own camp spot. As they approached, his sister Miriam—a tall woman with snowy hair and a tanned, wrinkled face—came out of her tent. Though Bezalel hadn't seen her for years, he recognized her regal air and remembered how, as a little boy, he had been in awe of her. As far back as he could remember, she had been known as a prophetess with unusual talents and insights.

She listened to Moses and the crowd for a while, then disappeared into her tent, coming back a few minutes later with a timbrel in her hand. In a voice that sounded much younger than one would expect from such a wrinkled visage, Miriam took up Moses' song.

Moses stopped, smiled broadly at his sister, and motioned to her with his hand as if to say, "It's your turn!"

"Sing to the Lord, for He is highly exalted," she began, taking up his refrain. She wove through the crowds as Moses had. This time the women followed her and soon Miriam led a throng of them. They danced through the camp as Moses and the men had, picking up followers as they went.

They made their way past Bezalel and he caught sight of his mother and Zamri in the crowd of dancers. It was good to see his mother so light-hearted, and Zamri able to express her naturally bubbly nature.

Of course there were others too, no lack of lovely women on which to feast one's eyes. Bezalel watched one, and then another, until he saw a delightful creature such as he had never seen before. She was a few women away from Zamri and had thick, wavy hair the color of copper. Her eyes, when they were open, flashed green malachite. Her skin was tanned, her face and lips flushed with exertion. Damp tendrils of hair clung to her face and neck. She was beautiful!

But more than her physical beauty attracted Bezalel. Fascinated, he watched her dance with abandon and not a shred of self-consciousness, as if performing for Yahweh Himself. Her movements were the exact physical expression of lightness and joy Bezalel had felt after he had removed his charm during the plague of darkness.

He had to find out who she was.

PART THREE

Wandering

CHAPTER

fifteen

"I SEE WATER UP AHEAD," EXCLAIMED ZAMRI FOR ABOUT THE SIXTH TIME since they had set out.

"It's not water," Uri said. "It's a trick our eyes play on us in the flat sand and sun. It's called a mirage, but if we keep walking we're sure to find water soon."

"I'm thirsty now," said Zamri. "Can I have a drink from your flask? Mine is empty."

Bezalel thought the whiney tone of her voice might cause their mother to deny her request, but Noemi replied, "Just a little drink." She rationed everyone's water every morning from their main supply. They replenished it at every possible water source. Their sheep and goat also needed to be watered from the jug.

It was two days since they had celebrated the Red Sea crossing. The very next day, the cloud had lifted, signifying it was time to move on, for that is what Moses had told them. They moved when it moved and stopped when it stopped.

They now traveled in a southerly direction through the Desert of Shur. The landscape was desolate. As far as the eye could see there was only sand, broken up by the occasional stunted juniper, hyssop, or giant anthill. The euphoria of the early days was replaced by gloomy resignation as the people faced the physical stresses of desert travel.

During the hours of walking, the family members often chatted with friends and old acquaintances they had lost touch with during the years of exhausting slavery. Noemi connected again with family members with whom she had grown up from the tribe of Dan.

Zamri was never happier than when she was chatting, giggling, teasing, and telling secrets to childhood friends Cetura and Sephora.

Bezalel often walked beside Shoshan. They discussed some of the projects they had made, though the days spent in Khafra's shop already seemed like something from the distant past. They also dreamed about the future. Maybe they would set up a shop of their own in the place they were going.

"Do you think people would give us commissions?" Bezalel asked.

"With you there, there's no doubt people would come," Shoshan said. "You can make anything."

"You flatterer," Bezalel said, feeling his face go hot, though Shoshan's words pleased him.

In all the walking and talking, Bezalel couldn't get the beautiful dancer out of his mind. He asked Zamri, "When you were dancing with Miriam the day after we crossed the sea, there was a girl about two or three away from you with wavy, copper-colored hair. Do you know who she is?"

"You mean the one with the Egyptian dress and fancy collar?" Zamri asked.

"Yes, that one."

"That's Sebia," said Zamri. "She's betrothed to Ethan."

Bezalel's heart fell.

* * *

When they camped on the second day, still having found no water, Noemi rationed the family to half their usual amount. By the end of the third day, an air of heaviness and anxiety was again rampant throughout the camp.

"You'd think Moses would have scouted out the water holes before he brought us out here," someone said.

"After the miracles he has performed, why can't he just make water appear?" someone else asked.

The comments around him fed Bezalel's own discontent. It was confusing. Why did Yahweh help them at some times but not at others?

"I'm so thirsty," said Zamri for about the tenth time since setting out that morning.

"Have a sip of my water," said Hur, "and don't despair. I'm sure after helping us escape the Egyptians, God won't let us die of thirst. We'll find water soon."

On the morning of the fourth day, the distant skyline appeared jagged. For once the shape on the horizon didn't disappear but grew larger and larger until they could make out what it was. Palm trees. A wadi. Water, at last!

But long before Bezalel's family got to the stream at the oasis, the news had filtered back. The water was bitter. Bezalel's own disappointment was expressed in Zamri's frustrated tears. "All I want is a drink," she sobbed.

In front and behind them, people muttered and grumbled.

"Our goats are already drying up. Soon we won't have milk, either."

"What will become of us in this heat without water?"

But Hur remained steadfast. "Yahweh has brought us here. He will not abandon us."

His words irritated Bezalel. Despite his change of heart, he still sometimes found his grandfather's optimism and simple faith maddening.

The family moved ahead with the crowd and came eventually to the groves of stately palms and clumps of junipers. They passed people setting up tents in the welcome shade. At least they had that.

Bezalel helped his father put up the tent in the spot they had picked out. Noemi still had flour and oil but needed fuel to bake bread, so he went in search of firewood.

As he scouted the outskirts of the camp, picking up dried juniper twigs, he met others doing the same. Everywhere he heard complaining, and he couldn't help but agree. What good was a leader who couldn't even take them to places with enough water?

He decided to go see the bitter water stream and joined the knot of people clustered on the bank. The water even looked unhealthy—brown and slow moving. He went to its edge, dipped in a finger, and brought it to his mouth. It was vile.

"This place is rightly called Marah," said someone, "for it's entirely a bitter disappointment."

Just then, Bezalel caught sight of Moses. He stood off to the side, eyes shut and an intent look on his face, as if he were listening. While Bezalel looked on, he saw Moses open his eyes, then walk toward the stream. People made way for him, opening up a path.

When he came to the edge of the water, he stooped down, dipped his finger in the stream, put it to his mouth as Bezalel had done, and grimaced. Then he fell to his knees and, raising his hands, looked skyward. The people around him became silent as he rocked gently forward and back, groaning as if from the bottom of his soul. Gradually he became still, then got to his feet and looked around.

"Bring me that limb," he said, pointing to a gnarled and thorny branch close to the stream's edge. The person nearest picked it up, brought it to Moses, and he threw it into the water.

Bezalel crowded close with the others, wondering what would appear. But there was nothing to see. The brown water gurgled on, over the twig and on toward its destination.

"Drink it now," said Moses.

A man knelt beside the water, cupped some in his hands, and brought it, dripping brown, to his mouth. As everyone looked on, he took a swallow. His face registered surprise. "It tastes fine," he said.

Bezalel's own mouth watered at the trickling sound of the stream, even as the color disgusted him. He went near, put down his firewood bundle, and also made a cup of his hands and drank. The water was cold, sweet, and good. Yahweh had helped them again!

He felt both reassured and annoyed with himself. He should have known this unpredictable God would stretch their trust until it was all but broken, then come through with a miracle in the nick of time.

He took another long drink before picking up the firewood and setting off for the camp to tell his family the good news.

CHAPTER

sixteen

BEZALEL SCANNED THE CROWD FOR THE FACE THAT HAD PREOCCUPIED him since the day of the Red Sea celebration. Even though Sebia was betrothed, he couldn't get her out of his mind. He didn't see her anywhere, however, so he turned his attention to Moses and Aaron, who had called an assembly of the people.

"You have drunk the waters of Marah," Moses said to Aaron, who repeated it to the crowd. "He has used it to cleanse you from the Egyptians' diseases."

Bezalel thought back to the weeks they had spent here and realized what Moses said was true. Zamri's skin, which had been pocked with pimples, had become clear and smooth. His father, who often had stomachaches, had reacted to the water strongly at first, but later his appetite improved and he said he felt better than he had in years.

Moses and Aaron continued, "From now on, listen carefully to His voice, the voice of Jehovah—Yahweh, the Lord your God—and do what is right in His eyes. If you pay attention to His commands and keep His decrees, He will shield you from chancres and boils, fevers and worms, stomach ailments and breathing problems. This is what He says: 'I will not bring on you any of the diseases I brought on the Egyptians, for I am the Lord who heals you.'"

Was Moses saying there was a connection between obeying God and physical health? There was so much about Yahweh that he didn't know.

* * *

"We'll not be thirsty here," said Zamri, kneeling down and drinking straight from one of the streams.

"Here, take a big drink!" said her friend Cetura, pushing her into the water.

"Bezalel needs a drink too," said Sephora, pushing him toward the stream. In a few minutes, everyone was thoroughly soaked and laughing.

After several weeks at Marah, the cloud had lifted and led them to this place—Elim. It was a verdant spot compared to other places they had camped at. Its twelve fresh water springs ensured there was plenty of water for all.

Bezalel was glad when the cloud stayed over this place day after day. They had been out of Egypt just over a month now, though it seemed much longer. If only this were the Promised Land, he thought. He was ready for this trip to be over.

In the first week of the month of Iyyar, Bezalel turned twenty. His family celebrated by inviting Bezalel's friends to eat a meal with them. Shoshan, Benjamin, and others from Khafra's shop were there, along with someone new—the son of one of his mother's girlhood friends. His name was Oholiab and his raven-haired wife Saria and their son, a three-year-old named Obed, accompanied him. Oholiab cut a colorful figure in his tunic, woven in a complicated pattern of red, blue, and gold. He laughed a lot and Bezalel took an instant liking to him.

The meal was like all the other meals they had eaten since leaving Egypt—bread dipped in oil and vinegar, lentil stew, and yogurt, with the addition of dates that Noemi had brought out in honor of the occasion. Oholiab distinguished himself with his hearty appetite and was still munching on dates long after everyone else was finished.

Bezalel found they had a lot in common, for Oholiab was also a craftsman and artist. "I worked for a time under Hori in the gem cutter's guild in Pi-Ramesses," he told Bezalel.

"So did I!" exclaimed Bezalel, though on comparing experiences, it was clear that Oholiab had worked in Hori's shop some years before Bezalel had come to Pi-Ramesses.

Oholiab went on to describe his work with Pharaoh's weavers. "We worked with the finest of linens, pleating it and decorating it with beads and feathers. Some pieces we dyed and made into sails and covers for canopies. We also made many baskets and mats in complex designs. Gorgeous pieces!"

"It sounds like you enjoyed your time as a weaver for Pharaoh," said Bezalel.

"Yes," said Oholiab. "At one time I would have been happy to stay and work for Pharaoh the rest of my life. Until Moses came back. After I saw the power of Yahweh, I wanted to follow Him alone. Once I wove fine robes for Pharaoh the god of Egypt. Now I would happily weave for Yahweh. But I don't think He needs my clothes." He said the last with a twinkle in his eye.

Oholiab's fanciful thoughts captured Bezalel's imagination. He too had once made beautiful things for Pharaoh and the Egyptian gods. What a novel idea—to do the same for Yahweh, the God he now served. But how could that be possible, since Yahweh was invisible?

The hours flew by as everyone talked and laughed. The sun was long set when the guests finally left. After bidding the last one farewell,

Bezalel lingered outside the tent. As he pulled his robe around him against the cold air, he still felt inner warmth. It was good to have met a fellow craftsman. They had a lot in common, even though their skills were different. Maybe someday, when they got to the Promised Land, Oholiab would also be a part of his and Shoshan's shop.

* * *

From his corner of the tent, Bezalel fished out the old robe that held his tools. He took the parcel to the light of the tent opening and unwrapped it. There they were—the mallet, bellows, tongs, crucible, wax, chisels, smoothing stone, awl, and knife. He hadn't used them since the fateful day of his confrontation with Khafra. The sight of them gave him the yen to get his hands on a piece of wood, gold, or electrum.

They had been camped at Elim for some time now and Bezalel couldn't remember when he had slept so soundly or so long. It was as if the excitement of leaving Pi-Ramesses, the escape from Egypt, the Red Sea crossing, and the long days of walking were exacting their toll in sleep. But now his energy was back and with it the desire to keep busy. He had missed the creative outlet that came from working with his hands. More than that, he needed to face a nagging question. Did he still possess his old skill, even without his amulet?

Leaving his tools, he walked around Elim searching for pieces of wood he could carve. Twisted limbs of acacia attracted his attention and he gathered a bundle. Back at the tent, he chose one in which he saw a potential sheep and was soon hard at work whittling with his knife.

"What are you making?" Zamri asked. She and her friends came over to watch.

"What do you think it is?" said Bezalel.

"It's a sheep," said Cetura.

"Remember when you made my doll?" asked Zamri. "I wish I still had it."

The girls watched as the animal took shape under Bezalel's hands. Soon other youths joined the crowd around him.

"How do you do that?" asked one boy.

"I'm not sure exactly," said Bezalel. "I just know that my eyes and my hands work together to make the things I see in my imagination. Would you like to try?"

He handed the knife and half-finished carving to the boy, who fumbled with them until Bezalel adjusted them in his hands. But when he tried to carve, the knife slipped on the hard wood and the carving popped out of his hand.

"It's not as easy as it looks," the boy said.

"Here, let me show you." Bezalel demonstrated how to hold the wood and the knife to get the best leverage. He explained how he decided where to remove the bits of wood to make a sheep and where to leave the block as it was.

More of the children asked for a turn at carving. Before he knew it, the sun was low in the sky and Noemi was calling him for the evening meal.

"Can we do this again?" the children asked as he gathered the tools and wood pieces.

"Sure," he said, "come back tomorrow. But bring your own knives or carving tools."

So began training in carving for the youth of the camp as Bezalel spent the next days trying to figure out how to teach them skills he couldn't recall ever having learned.

seventeen

"The anniversary of our marriage is near and I would like to give Sharia something special made of gold," Oholiab said. It was several weeks after Bezalel's birthday and Oholiab had returned to Bezalel's tent carrying a small linen bundle. Now he untied it to reveal a collection of gleaming trinkets. "Could you recast something? I'd like to make her a necklace. I have the chain, but I want a pendant that isn't inscribed with Egyptian magic. I will pay you well."

Bezalel fingered the pile of amulets, necklaces, bracelets, and rings. They were shaped and inscribed with scarabs, eyes of Horus, and ankhs.

Just looking at them brought back memories of his years in Khafra's shop and the feelings of confusion he had once felt about God.

"What shape would you like me to make?" he asked.

"Something that speaks of love," said Oholiab. "I think a pomegranate. It's her favorite fruit."

It had been a while since Bezalel had done any gold casting. Without the amulet, would he still have the skill? Would he be able to find the materials he needed here in the desert?

He chose the gold for his project, careful to pick pieces similar in color and quality. Then he sent Zamri to fetch Shoshan, who had a spare shovel. Meanwhile Bezalel got his tools, his own shovel, some water, and several brick molds his family had brought with them. When Shoshan arrived, Zamri and two of her friends helped carry the supplies to the edge of camp.

They selected an area near a flat stone which Bezalel could use as a worktable. He recruited Oholiab, Zamri, and her friends to gather dry grass and weeds while he and Shoshan went in search of clay.

After several digs below the sandy topsoil, they found the dense, sticky earth they needed. Bezalel squeezed and worked the substance in his hands. It didn't have the consistency of the clay they had used in Khafra's shop—the clay Khafra had perfected and of which only he knew the formula. Would this raw desert clay work? It would certainly serve well for kiln bricks, but would it work as a mold for a finely crafted trinket? He would have to give it a try.

Shoshan and Bezalel dug shovelfuls of clay and brought them to where Oholiab and the girls had collected weeds and grass. When they had enough, they dampened the clay, combined it with the plant material, and soon the girls were laughing and dancing around the wet brick mud as they mixed it with their feet, just as they had in Egypt.

By now others had gathered to watch. When it was time to fill the brick molds with clay, a few onlookers must have gone to their tents to provide more molds, for soon twelve bricks were drying in the sun.

Bezalel untied his collection of tools and took out the ball of beeswax. It had softened in the day's heat and he easily separated a segment of it.

"About this size?" he asked.

Oholiab gave his assent and Bezalel began pressing and forming the wax into the shape of a pomegranate. How wonderful it felt to again model the wax. The form quickly took shape in his hands. It was as if his fingers had their own knowledge of what to do.

After Bezalel had formed the pomegranate, he used a stylus to etch details—the puckers at the stem end and one half of the fruit open, showing its layer of rind and clusters of fat round seeds. Finally, he was satisfied that it was finished.

He then chose a piece of pure clay and softened it with a little water. He squeezed and pressed it, feeling for and removing pebbles, bits of root, or plant material—anything that wasn't clay. When it was as clean as he could make it, he took up the wax pomegranate and smothered it in clay, careful to force mud into every crack and fissure of its shape. He left two holes at the top.

"Why are you doing that?" asked Zamri.

"I'm making a mold," said Bezalel. "When we put this into the fire, the wax will burn away and only the clay will be left. Then I'll pour the gold into the big hole, and the little hole will let the air escape. That's all we can do today. The bricks and the pomegranate must dry before we can fire them."

A few days later, the bricks were dry. Bezalel and Shoshan then built a hot bonfire and fired the bricks. When the fire finally died down, though two had shattered, they had ten perfect bricks with which to build a kiln to melt Oholiab's gold.

A small crowd gathered to watch Bezalel do the casting a few days later. On the ground, Bezalel had built a square kiln with the fired bricks. Shards of the broken bricks made a low platform for the fuel of twigs. There was even a place to nest his crucible.

"We need lots of wood for the fire, right?" asked Zamri.

"Not as much as you might think," replied Bezalel. "When we fired the bricks, the grass and weeds we mixed in the clay burned out, leaving tiny air pockets. Those pockets help the bricks hold much heat. Still, it'll get pretty warm. You won't want to stand too close."

While the fire burned, Bezalel placed the clay-covered pomegranate into the crucible and nestled it in its place between the pieces of brick. Bezalel fed the fire and Shoshan worked the bellows so that it burned hotter and hotter.

His years of working in Khafra's shop gave Bezalel the sense of when the clay had been in the fire long enough. Had it survived the firing? Would he have a usable mold, or would he have to start all over again?

When the fire had cooled, Bezalel took his tongs, grasped the crucible with its precious clay mold, removed it from the kiln, and studied it. Of course the wax was gone now, consumed by the fire. The form that was left behind looked to be in perfect shape. The clay had worked! He transferred it ever so gently onto the stone worktable.

A few hours later, after the mold was cool enough to accept the molten gold, Bezalel lay the trinkets Oholiab had given him into the crucible. His heart raced. Working with gold was the part he loved the most!

Again Bezalel and Shoshan fed the fire twigs of juniper and acacia until the heat drove everyone back. When Bezalel sensed the kiln was hot enough, he placed the crucible, now with its precious load of pure gold, into the flames. Every once in a while, he pulled it out with the tongs to check on its progress. Finally it melted into a smooth, glittering liquid.

Ever so delicately, he poured the molten metal from the crucible into the large hole of the mold. When the gold cooled a little, he put it back into the fire to heat again. Back and forth he went, pouring a little, heating, then pouring again.

At last, the mold was full.

"How do we get it out?" asked Zamri.

"We don't for a while," said Bezalel. "It needs to cool first. We'll cover it with sand so it doesn't cool too quickly."

The next morning, Bezalel retrieved the clay mold from the sand. It was completely cool now and he could carry it in his hands.

As he took up his mallet, onlookers pressed close. He tapped the clay and it cracked, breaking away to reveal a pomegranate. It looked exactly like the one he had shaped from wax, only this one gleamed.

The shell of the fruit was smooth as still water with only a couple o nicks, and he could polish those away. The part showing the inside w an intricate filigree of seeds attached to the rind. Even the tab for t chain hole was intact.

Bezalel felt a thrill of accomplishment and great relief. Remo' the Egyptian amulet hadn't changed anything. He still had skill.

"It's gorgeous!" someone said.

"I'd like one of those," said another.

Bezalel drilled the chain hole, polished and cleaned the trink it shone, then handed it to Oholiab.

"It looks good enough to eat," said Oholiab, taking the jewe one hand and patting his rounded stomach with the other. " know what I'd give to sink my teeth into one of these."

"You and your perpetual hunger," Bezalel said, giving his frienu a playful punch on the shoulder.

* * *

Words of Bezalel's project soon spread around the camp. Over the next few days, others came to him with requests to make jewelry pieces in the shapes of pomegranates, apples, figs, and leaves.

When Bezalel and Shoshan couldn't keep up with the demand, Shoshan spread the word among other craftsmen who had worked at various craft shops in Egypt to come and assist. Despite the number of workmen that soon assembled, Bezalel couldn't help but notice he was the first craftsman most people requested when they came with their orders. He hadn't lost his touch. It felt good to again be singled out and praised for his talent.

* * *

"What are we doing out here again?"
"Where are we going to get food?"

91

"What are we going to eat?"

"Remember Egypt? There we had meat and all the food we wanted. I wish we were back there."

Bezalel and the other craftsmen had just got their workshop established when the cloud lifted and moved on, away from lush Elim. "Maybe we'll finally reach Canaan this time," some of the people said hopefully as they packed their belongings and again set out.

The cloud led them back into the vast desert called the Wilderness of Sin, exposing them to familiar hardships. Now, after only a day of travel, the camp was already buzzing with discontent.

In Bezalel's family, no one voiced complaints. Hur wouldn't allow it. But Bezalel watched his mother's furrowed brow and abrupt motions as she moved from her cooking fire to the tent, preparing their meager meal. She looked as upset and irritated as the loudest complainers.

Bezalel struggled with discontented thoughts himself. Surely he'd have been better off in Khafra's workshop where all his food was supplied and the most beautiful woods and finest gold and gems were plentiful.

Then he remembered the long night when he had promised Yahweh his life. The moment he had broken the chain of Ptah's amulet, he had severed his tie with Egypt. He couldn't go back, neither did he want to.

As for complaining now, he thought back to just a few weeks ago when he had grumbled about Moses with the others. He had felt so foolish when Moses again gave them water at Marah. He would try to be more like Grandpa Hur and resist voicing the discontent he felt.

However, the grumbling all around was impossible to ignore. The air was heavy with it. One morning, when some were on the verge of forsaking camp and turning to go back to Egypt, Aaron's messengers announced an assembly.

Bezalel dreaded the confrontation he knew was about to take place. He felt like staying in the camp, but Hur urged him to come. "Don't underestimate God or Moses," he said. "God has seen us through to this point. Surely He won't forsake us now."

The crowd gathered in front of Moses and Aaron. As at other times, Moses spoke to Aaron and Aaron relayed Moses' message to the people.

"Come before the Lord, for He has heard your grumbling," Aaron began. "These are the words of Yahweh to you. 'I have heard the grumbling of the Israelites. Tell them at twilight you will eat meat and in the morning you will be filled with bread. Then you will know that I am the Lord your God.'"

Sarcasm and mocking filled the air around Bezalel.

"Sure, sure. God will rain down meat?"

"Did you hear that? 'This evening,' he says. What a joke!"

Perhaps it was the audacity of the mockery or its widespread presence throughout the camp. Whatever it was, Moses himself spoke out now.

"You will know that it is the Lord when He really does give you meat in the evening and bread in the morning. Yahweh has heard your grumbling. For it is against Him, not us. You aren't grumbling against Aaron and me, you are grumbling against Yahweh Himself."

As his words rang out across the crowd, the people stopped muttering to each other and a guilty silence hung over the camp. Bezalel felt convicted. Though he hadn't spoken his complaints aloud, his mind had been full of them.

Now Aaron continued. "Yahweh has said, 'You will see the glory of the Lord.' Look!" He pointed toward the sky over the desert, toward the cloud that hung there motionless.

Bezalel looked in that direction and, as he gazed, he saw the cloud glow brighter and brighter until his eyes couldn't stand the light and he had to look away. Around him he saw that the sight stunned others too. Instead of snide comments and mockery, there was silence.

"In the morning, the Lord will rain down bread," Aaron went on. "You are to go out each day and gather enough for that day. On the sixth day, bring in twice as much as you gather on the other days. That way you will be able to observe Shabbat as a day of rest. Follow these instructions. They are God's test for you. Now go. Prepare for meat at twilight and bread in the morning."

As Bezalel's family made their way back to the tent, Bezalel wondered how God would keep His promise.

The day wore on and he found himself scanning the horizon, though he chided himself. Even the biggest band of traders imaginable couldn't carry enough meat for their thousands. Despite knowing this, the closer evening came, the more he watched, until *there was something*. It looked like a cloud, but then it changed into a gigantic flock of birds. It grew larger until they were overhead. Then they descended right into the camp.

Quail. Plump and healthy but unexplainably easy to catch. Bezalel, Zamri, Uri, and Hur caught two dozen in no time. Noemi took the fluttering birds by their legs, slaughtered, defeathered, and dressed them. Soon the smell of roasting meat filled the air. Throughout the camp, others were doing the same thing.

Bezalel couldn't remember when meat had tasted so good. He went to sleep feeling full and content.

The next morning, he awoke to excited chatter outside the tent. "Frost… wafers… honey…"

He got up to discover that Noemi was gone.

"Where's Mother?" he asked Hur, who was sitting outside the tent meditating and praying, as was his morning custom.

"She has gone outside the camp with the others to collect the bread we were promised yesterday," said Hur.

Bezalel had forgotten about that. Moses had promised bread in the morning in addition to the meat at night. "I'm going too," he said, trotting through the camp toward open land which was now crowded with people and their baskets.

On the ground he saw a white substance. It looked like frost. He reached down and picked some up. It crumbled in his hands like the most fragile and brittle unleavened bread. He put it in his mouth and felt it dissolve on his tongue. It was sweet like honey and tasted of coriander.

"What is it?" he asked someone who was collecting it beside him.

"You tell me," the person said. "Manna. What is it?"

Bezalel ate until he was full. Then he gathered more into the folds of his cloak. He stayed out until, under the hot sun, the miraculous food melted away. He had been right to trust Moses and God. But would he ever learn to do it without fighting doubts and questions every step of the way?

CHAPTER

eighteen

"Zamri, it's time to get up. The sun is already warm and you still haven't gone for the manna." Noemi's voice was urgent.

From behind the tent partition, Bezalel heard Zamri groan and mutter, "I don't have to. I collected extra yesterday."

A minute later, Bezalel heard his mother exclaim, "Oh no! This is awful!"

As he pulled on his tunic and tied his robe around him, Bezalel detected a smell of decay and rottenness. He went over to the basket of yesterday's manna, looked inside, then drew back, repulsed. The food that had been deliciously edible the day before now stank and was crawling with maggots. It was disgusting.

Hur, hearing the fuss inside the tent, came in to see what it was about.

"It's yesterday's manna," said Noemi. "Zamri collected extra without telling us. Today it smells and is full of worms."

Zamri was up by now, fully awakened by everyone's reaction to what she'd done.

"Didn't you hear Moses' command?" Hur asked. "We are to collect only enough for each day, no more."

"My friends did it too," said Zamri. "We wanted to sleep today."

"Well, we'd better get out there now," said Noemi. "The sun is already high in the sky. You know how the heat melts it."

"I'll help," said Bezalel. He dumped the spoiled manna outside the tent, but the odor lingered on the basket, so he left it outside and found another. Then he joined Noemi and the other manna-gatherers already sweating in the warm morning sun.

He went a distance from the others, where the supply was still untouched, and began filling the basket. It was a pleasant, easy job and he soon found his thoughts wandering again to the strange existence that had become his life. Who would have thought, even a few weeks ago, that he would be out here collecting this strange food and no longer doing what had been his whole life from as far back as he could remember?

His mind drifted to Pi-Ramesses and Khafra's shop. Right now they would be starting the day's work. He wondered how Khafra's son had fared. Killed with the other firstborn sons, he guessed. That would have broken Khafra's heart. And what about Karem? Had Khafra found someone else for the bold young woman? He could think of four or five workmen who would be delighted with the offer he had received.

His thoughts interrupted by the sound of approaching footsteps. He looked up to see a girl looking down at him—a girl with wavy, auburn hair and green-black eyes. A smile played around her mouth. Sebia!

"Shalom," she said.

Bezalel jumped to his feet, his face instantly burning hot and his mouth dry. He gave her a nod. "Shalom," he said.

"I see there is plenty of manna here. Do you mind if I join you?"

"Of course not," said Bezalel. He let his eyes flit over her before raising them again to her face. At close range, she was even more beautiful than he remembered. But he didn't know what to say, so he bent down and resumed filling his basket.

She began working beside him and then broke the silence. "Are you the one who makes things out of gold?"

"I have done that," said Bezalel.

"I thought you were the one," Sebia said. "A cousin of an acquaintance worked with you in Elim. Abnosh is his name."

"I don't recall him."

"He told us about you. When I heard of your skill, I wanted to meet you and ask you to make a gift for my mother. You're Bezalel, right?"

"Yes, Bezalel, son of Uri from the tribe of Judah." Bezalel was surprised she knew so much about him.

"I am Sebia, from the tribe of Naphtali. My father is Jahzer of the Jahzeelites. I know my mother would love one of your pieces," she said. "Could you make her a bracelet if I got the materials? I will pay you well."

"Of course," said Bezalel, feeling more comfortable all the time. Then, realizing that his basket was overflowing while hers still had plenty of room, he began placing manna into her basket. They worked side by side in silence for a little while. When she had collected enough, they picked up their respective loads and walked back toward the camp together.

"I'm glad I met you," said Sebia as they reached the camp outskirts. "Could I bring the gold tomorrow? Will you be here again?"

Would he! "Yes, I'll be here again."

They parted and Bezalel walked back to their tent, but later couldn't remember how he had gotten there. He had met Sebia! He was going to make her mother a gift. He would see her again tomorrow.

Bezalel delivered the basket to Noemi, who had already been back for a few minutes and was working with the manna. "How do you want it this morning?" she asked Bezalel.

"However you like," he said, his mind still in a fog.

"You're easy to please," she said.

She sang as she placed each handful of manna into a pottery bowl and crushed it fine as meal with a stone pestle. Predictable daily food together with the challenge of cooking it in different ways had transformed Noemi into a happy, contented woman again.

"I think it will be baked cakes this morning," she said.

"Great." Bezalel slipped a wafer from the basket into his mouth, then went outside to where Hur sat in his usual spot.

"Were the people lining up to see Moses?" Hur asked.

"I didn't notice."

"Well, I've heard he has taken to sitting for hours sorting out the people's problems. That's something I would like to witness."

Shortly Uri came back from tending the animals and the family sat down to eat. After everyone was satisfied, Hur announced, "I'm going to the gathering place to watch Moses judge the people. Uri, Bezalel, I think you should join me."

When they arrived at the area that served as the camp's meeting place, it was indeed as Hur had said. The queue of people waiting to speak to Moses stretched through the center of the natural amphitheater and beyond, past several clusters of tents. The three found a spot with other onlookers where they could hear and watch the proceedings. People came with a variety of matters.

One man complained that a neighbor was making advances toward his wife. Others brought charges of theft, trespass, and annoying, noisy neighbors. "My neighbor's extra manna smells so terrible we can't sleep," said a man who had just reached Moses.

Aaron, who sat beside Moses and did most of the speaking, answered. "You bother Moses with a small matter like that? Just ask your neighbor to take it away…"

But Moses flashed Aaron a quick frown and broke in. "This may seem like a small matter, but it isn't. Is your neighbor here?"

When the complainant pointed out the man, Moses spoke to him in a surprisingly harsh tone. "I told you—in fact, I made it very clear—that no one is to keep any of the manna until morning. What about that command do you not understand? Collect enough for one day and one day only."

Looking around at the people gathered, Moses proclaimed to everyone, "People, listen to what God says and obey Him for a change. Why do you keep cutting corners and not doing exactly as He says?"

Bezalel was surprised at Moses' reaction. Was disobedience in such a small thing that big of a problem? It seemed that Yahweh demanded compliance down to the last detail. He also felt a wave of relief. It was a good thing their day-old manna matter had been dealt with this morning and within their tent.

But what about other things in which Moses judged the people? Sebia, for example. If she were truly betrothed to someone else, he would need to be very careful in his relationship with her. He didn't want to be the object of God's wrath delivered through Moses' fiery gaze.

"REMEMBER MOSES' COMMAND ABOUT THE SHABBAT," HUR SAID TO Bezalel and Zamri before they went out to do their collection the next morning. "You are to collect double the amount of manna and eat the extra portion on Shabbat."

"That's right," said Noemi. "Take the large baskets."

They went to the place they had worked the day before. Again Bezalel went off by himself, as near to the place he had been yesterday as possible but still far enough away from the other gatherers so that when Sebia came, they would be alone. He tried to concentrate on his work but caught himself glancing up again and again. At last, when he had almost filled the first basket, he saw her in the distance. He busied himself but still sneaked a couple of quick looks to make sure it really was she.

"Shalom," she said, reaching into her basket and taking out a cloth parcel. "Here is the gold."

"What design do you want?" asked Bezalel. He barely trusted himself to look into her eyes. Yet when he finally did, he couldn't take his gaze away and his eyes clung to hers as if to a magnet.

"Hmmm," she said, the first to look down, "make them into some kind of flower. She loves almond flowers. Could you make a bracelet in a series of almond blossoms?"

"Yes," said Bezalel. He put the parcel in the bottom of the second basket and began filling it.

"Two baskets today?" asked Sebia.

"Tomorrow is the Sabbath," Bezalel said. "Remember, Moses said to collect double so it can be a day of rest."

"Right," said Sebia. "I'd better hurry and get this full so I have time to get another."

"I'll help you," said Bezalel. He began filling her basket, even though his second was only one-third full. He felt giddy working by her side. Their hands brushed together once when they threw in handfuls of manna at the same time. The touch sparked a shiver through his whole body.

Calm down, he told himself. But the pounding in his chest and the sweatiness of his hands continued.

"You're getting all gummed up," said Sebia, pointing to his white-crusted hands and laughing. She seemed unaware of his discomfort.

He looked down at the guilty culprits. "I guess it's the heat," he said. He could feel how red his face must have looked.

"You're quiet today," said Sebia.

Bezalel tried to think what to choose, from the confusion of his thoughts, to say to her. If he asked her outright whether she was betrothed to someone else, she might think him forward and inappropriate. And if she were, of course their relationship, as he envisioned it, would end right then and there. But if he said nothing and carried on as if they were simply friends, was that fair to her, especially given the way he felt?

She broke the silence again. "What do you think of Moses coming to lead us out of Egypt? What do you think of this?" She gestured to indicate their camp and the surrounding desert.

"I think Moses is a great man," said Bezalel. "What he did, and what he is doing—someday we'll tell our children about it and it will still seem amazing. I worked in one of Pharaoh's craft shops. I didn't have to work at hard labor like my family did. The Egyptians made even my little sister work many hours a day. I know Moses' coming was God's plan for us."

"Me too," said Sebia. "I prayed to Him and He answered my prayer. I will do whatever Yahweh says. I believe He sent Moses."

Her candor made Bezalel brave—maybe even foolhardy? Whatever it was, he realized that more than anything else he wanted their friendship on an honest footing.

"You asked me a moment ago why I was quiet," Bezalel said. "It's because I was thinking. About us. I was watching Moses judge the people yesterday. A man came with the complaint that his wife was unfaithful to him. Moses was very definite about the seriousness of unfaithfulness." He looked at Sebia now, his eyes straight into hers. "Sebia, are you involved with anyone? Are you betrothed to someone in marriage?"

She looked down as if unable to face his question and his heart plummeted. Then she faced him again full on. "Ethan, son of Dathan of the tribe of Zebulun, has asked for my hand in marriage. My parents are waiting for my answer. They want me to say yes. Ethan's father has influence and they say my marrying Ethan would be an honor. But up until now I have put them off. I don't know… I don't know if I want to marry."

She said that last so quietly that Bezalel wasn't sure he had heart her right.

"Of course you'll marry," he said. Her humble manner was endearing and there was still hope for him, though asking her to go against the wishes of her parents? It wasn't a thought he relished. "I asked because I first saw you dancing with Miriam and the women the day we crossed the Red Sea. When I talked to my sister about you, she said you were betrothed."

"Ethan tells everyone that," said Sebia. Now her face was as red as his had felt a few minutes before, and she wouldn't meet his gaze.

They walked back to the camp in silence and parted with a simple farewell. Before he took the baskets into the tent, Bezalel fished out the parcel Sebia had given him. Now it was more important than ever to make the bracelet for Sebia's mother as beautiful as it could be.

* * *

That morning, after Noemi's meal of boiled manna, Bezalel joined Hur and Uri to watch and listen as Moses continued to judge the people.

"How does he do it?" asked Uri in amazement after watching Moses carry on for two and a half hours without a break.

"I would grow impatient with all the pettiness," said Hur. The men listened as Moses gave a judgment to two families disputing about the same camp spot, then called for the next complaint.

It turned out to be a group of people. Their spokesman introduced himself as Dathan, a leader of the tribe of Zebulun. Bezalel's ears pricked up. That must be the Dathan Sebia had told him about—the father of Ethan, who wanted to marry her.

Dathan began with an air of formality and almost obsequious politeness. "Oh noble Moses," he said, "we heard you say that each morning everyone is to gather just enough manna for the day. But this morning we saw many with double the amount of baskets, gathering twice as much as usual. What do you say to that?"

There was a smug smile on his face, and he stepped back as if expecting the sparks to fly.

And fly they did—though Bezalel was sure the result was not quite what he had anticipated.

Moses took a deep breath, as if trying to calm himself. Then, with exasperation heavy in his voice, he said, "This is exactly what they're supposed to do. As I told you all before, we are to keep the Sabbath by gathering twice as much on the day before so we can rest on the seventh day. This is as Yahweh has commanded. Your complaint shows you to be guilty of not listening to instructions. God help us if you truly are a leader. You need ears that are attentive to Him before you deserve to lead the people. Now go and prepare for a hungry Shabbat, as you obviously don't have extra food collected. Next."

As Moses scolded Dathan, Bezalel watched the expression on his face change from smugness, to surprise, to anger. Despite his natural antipathy to the man as the father of his rival, Bezalel felt sorry for him too. How embarrassing to get a tongue lashing like Moses had just given, and in front of everyone. But the incident also planted fear and respect inside him. How awful to offend this fiery representative of Yahweh.

Bezalel, Uri, and Hur watched for a bit longer, then went home. Their walk to the tent was unusually quiet. Bezalel was thinking of what he had just seen.

"What did you make of that?" he asked finally, breaking the silence.

"Moses is absolutely right," said Hur. "I only wish he wouldn't lose his temper. There's enough discontent in the camp without fostering more with anger and belittling people like Dathan. He has a big mouth and a big following. We haven't seen the end of this."

CHAPTER

twenty

"Why are we out here without water again?"

"Why didn't Moses tell us before we left what this would be like?"

"Oh, for the good old days in Egypt where we never even gave water a second thought."

Bezalel heard grumbling all around him as he trudged on. He had barely begun working on the bracelet for Sebia's mother when the cloud had lifted a week ago. He and the other craftsmen had had to pack up their tools.

It had been a week of walking over sandy plains and around stony outcrops. The vegetation was sparse, with scrubby grass, the occasional stunted juniper shrub, and once in a while a wild acacia. For the most part the surroundings were monotonous, the walk hot, dusty, and exhausting.

Traveling gave Bezalel mixed feelings. Whenever they set out, he felt excited. They were on their way again. Surely that meant that one of these days—weeks, at the most—they would end up at their destination, wonderful Canaan.

But this leg of the journey hadn't taken them there. At least not yet. Travel days were uncomfortable, tiring, and even dangerous. Sand fleas, disturbed by the multitude of feet, hovered near the ground and inflicted impossibly itchy bites on feet and ankles. Everyone had to be constantly alert for vipers, scorpions, and poisonous spiders. Vultures circled overhead, reminding them that foxes and jackals were even now tracking their progress. Their pace through this desolate place was slow to accommodate the children and animals, so they were easy targets.

There were also desert tribes who considered the land they were traveling through personal territory. So far there hadn't been any standoffs, though travelers on camels and bands of nomads had appeared in the distance from time to time.

And of course there was the everlasting need to find water. Sometimes they passed by small oases where they could replenish their water supply. But then would come long stretches without it when complaints and muttering were everywhere.

To take his mind off his thirst, Bezalel thought about Sebia. Where in the multitude did her family travel? And was she still undecided about Ethan? When they stopped and he could work on her mother's project again, he would stretch it out as long as he could. That way he wouldn't have to face the possibility that their friendship might be over.

* * *

One day, the cloud halted at a rocky place with a few dusty palms. Word went around that the place was called Rephidim.

"Why are we stopping here? There's not a stream in sight."

"What are we supposed to drink? Sand?"

As the people set up their tents and the grumbling continued, Bezalel fought the urge to join in. It was hard to stay even-tempered when he was tired to the bone, thirsty to distraction, and all the hopes of camping in a watered, green spot had been dashed by another dry stop.

He finished helping Uri put up the tent, and had just rewarded himself with the tiniest sip from his water skin when he saw a group of men stride by, their voices raised in angry conversation.

"He has to realize we've had enough!"

"I won't go another day watching my kids go thirsty."

"We will hold him responsible for any deaths!"

Bezalel was sure he saw Dathan in the group. It looked like the anger was finally going to boil over.

Uri and Hur, who had also witnessed the group, looked at each other. "Looks like trouble for Moses," said Hur. "Let's go to support Moses. He may need our help."

Bezalel hesitated. The men were very angry. Did he want to be seen with Hur and his father on Moses' side against the furious mob?

"Don't be afraid," said Hur, as if reading his mind. "Yahweh can handle even this angry crowd."

The confrontation was sharp and ugly. Dathan, for he indeed was with the men, confronted Moses as the spokesman for the dissidents. He stood inches from Moses and glared at him, his own face red and contorted with rage.

"We demand water," Dathan said. "Why are we stopping here? There's no water. What's your plan? Or maybe we should ask, do you even have a plan? It's your intention for us to all die in the desert, isn't it?"

Some of the men had picked up stones and now lifted them, as if threatening to throw them at Moses. Despite the surprise of the attack and the ferocity of the men, Moses didn't seem intimidated, or if he was, he didn't show any sign of it. Instead he shot back, "Why do you quarrel with me? Why do you put the Lord to the test?"

How would the men answer that, Bezalel wondered? He realized that was what Moses often did—deflected criticism away from himself to make it sound like the critic was finding fault with Yahweh. It silenced the men this time, as it had before. They stepped back, and though Bezalel heard the muttering and grumbling continue, they dropped their rocks.

"Go back to your tents," Moses said. "I'll let you know when I hear from God."

Despite the way Moses had defused the situation, the tension in the camp remained palpable.

"Moses doesn't listen to us. He's only in this for himself."

"We need a leader who understands us and will show some sympathy."

"This was such a bad idea. Let's turn around and go back to Egypt.

Despite his attempts to shut them out, Bezalel found their mutterings resonated with his own thoughts.

But Hur remained a rock of loyalty in their home. He squelched any talk of criticism. That evening, he even reprimanded Zamri when she started whining about being thirsty. "Don't complain," he said. "You're alive, aren't you? You have manna to eat every morning. As Moses always reminds us, complaining about our circumstances is complaining against Yahweh. He has never yet let us down."

Bezalel spent a restless night. Next morning, he was awakened early by conversation outside the tent. Hur, who always rose at first light, came in a few minutes later.

"Moses has summoned all the leaders of Israel," he whispered to Bezalel, who had sat up as he entered the tent. "He has asked me to come. I want you to come with me to see what Yahweh will do."

Bezalel and Hur arrived at the spot where the malcontents had met with Moses the day before. Many elders had already gathered. When everyone was assembled, Moses led the leaders away from the gathering crowd toward a huge rock. Bezalel watched as they stopped near it and backed away a few paces, as if instructed by Moses.

Then Moses took his rod in his hand—the one with which he had performed the signs in Egypt—and, with a dramatic motion, hit the rock.

Instantly a gush of water spewed from it, showering Moses and splattering the leaders, who retreated further. Realizing what had happened, they moved close, cupped their hands to catch the welcome liquid, and drank deep.

Bezalel felt as if a weight had been lifted from his shoulders. He heaved a huge sigh of relief. Yahweh had helped them again. Grandpa Hur's faith had not been misplaced.

As he and his grandfather hurried back to the camp to get their water jugs, Grandpa Hur began singing Moses' Red Sea song. "Who among the gods is like You, O Lord? Who is like You, majestic in holiness, awesome in glory, working wonders?"

Bezalel hummed along. But in the back of his mind were nagging thoughts. Though he hadn't voiced his thoughts, he had again been on the side of the complainers. Would his faith in Yahweh ever be strong enough to trust Him on his own?

CHAPTER

twenty-one

"Is there someone named Bezalel here?"

For the third time since he'd set to work this morning, Bezalel was interrupted. "I'm Bezalel," he said to the young man. "What would you like?"

"I have seen the things you make out of gold," the man said. "Could you cast something for my wife out of these?" He untied the cloth parcel he was carrying to reveal a variety of trinkets.

"I have a few projects ahead of yours," Bezalel said. "If you don't mind a wait, I can do it in a while."

As he returned to his work with the man's parcel, he thought about how good it felt to be working with his hands again. The many requests for his work meant that he'd be busy for a long time, even while collecting a little gold of his own.

The number of craftsmen had grown from when they had first set up their workspace at Elim. Skilled smiths and carvers, along with those just learning the craft, welcomed this opportunity to fill the long days with work that also gave them a way to amass wealth for the time they arrived at their new home.

Abnosh, the goldsmith Sebia had spoken of, had joined them again, along with several friends of his who had worked in a temple in Memphis. Their workstation was near his and, as he resumed his task, he overheard their conversation.

"It was good to get our water jugs filled again!" said one of Abnosh's friends.

"Amazing thing, Moses getting water from a rock. I heard he simply hit it and out it came," said another.

"But what do you make of Moses' leadership?" asked Abnosh. "My uncle Dathan says he's a disaster. He has no plan. Every day a new crisis, for which he needs another miracle."

Uncle Dathan! Had he heard right, Bezalel wondered? Then Abnosh must be Ethan's cousin. Ethan must have been the acquaintance Sebia referred to when she first told him about Abnosh. And he shared his uncle's low opinion of Moses. Bezalel was glad he hadn't told anyone whom his project was for. Suddenly the desert craft shop didn't seem like such a safe and welcoming place.

* * *

Now that they were no longer traveling and Bezalel's help was no longer needed with packing the tent and caring for the animals, he offered to go out to collect manna again. He told himself it was to help Zamri, though in his heart he knew he really did it with the hope of seeing Sebia again.

The second day he went out, he was rewarded. She surprised him as she came up silently behind him, touched him lightly on his back, and greeted him.

"Shalom."

He looked up at her—her beautiful face, her lovely shape. Even in his imagination she was never as gorgeous as in real life. He didn't answer her. As usual when she was around, he felt awkward and tongue-tied.

"How have you been?" she asked.

"Good," he said. "Thirsty. But now we have water. And you?"

"My family is well, but things are tense at home. Father is pressuring me for an answer about Ethan."

"What will you say?" asked Bezalel. He realized his own heart was thumping as he considered what her answer could mean to him.

"Part of me wants to say yes," said Sebia. "It would make Father and Mother so happy to have it settled. But I'm also afraid."

"Afraid of what?"

"That it will be a mistake. That I will regret it."

"Why would you regret it—if your parents and his approve, and he is a good man from a respected family, what is there to regret?" He couldn't believe he was encouraging her to accept Ethan's proposal. Still, she looked so distressed…

"I don't know Ethan well," said Sebia. "What I do suspect about him is that he wants me for what he sees. But I don't think he likes who I am."

Bezalel couldn't imagine anyone not liking her for any reason. "How do you mean?"

"I think I'm too expressive and impulsive for him," she said. "Remember the dance with Miriam after we crossed the Red Sea?"

"How could I forget?"

"See," she said, "you noticed it too. I was dancing my thanks to Yahweh that day, but Ethan said I made a fool of myself. He told my parents—well, they heard it through his parents, of course—that he would make a lady out of me."

"But that's what I liked about you," said Bezalel. "It was your worship of Yahweh with your whole self that caught my attention. It filled me with happiness. It reminded me of the day…" He stopped. He had never told anyone of his prayer to Yahweh during the three-day Egyptian night.

But she begged him to continue. "Which day? Tell me, please."

So he told her of his time in Khafra's shop and how he had once dreamed of gaining freedom for his family with his skill. But then Moses had come, and with him the plagues.

"As the plagues continued, it got worse and worse for us Hebrews," he said. "Finally, during the three days of darkness, I felt like I would be trapped in Egypt forever unless I chose Yahweh. That night, after I put my trust in God and removed my Egyptian charm, I felt light and free—exactly like you looked when you danced."

"That's beautiful, Bezalel," she said. "It helps me feel I'm not crazy, or showing off and trying to attract attention, as my parents and Ethan seem to think. Because I too have a reason for my love and loyalty to Yahweh. Someday I will tell you. But now I'd better get to work."

Bezalel wanted to hear her story now, but the sun was high and she had hardly any manna in her basket. It would have to wait. Bezalel collected manna by her side and they worked in silence, filling up both their containers.

When they were done, they started walking back toward the camp. "Should we be seen together?" asked Bezalel. "I don't want to get you into trouble."

"We're friends," she said, "and I'm happy to be seen with you. Ethan doesn't own me, even though he thinks he does. More and more I am leaning toward saying no to this betrothal."

Her words made Bezalel's heart sing.

Just before they parted, he remembered the almost-finished bracelet. "The gift for your mother is nearly finished," he said. "If you come out two days from now, I'll bring it with me and you can take it home."

After they parted, Bezalel felt like skipping back to the tent. He would see Sebia again in two days!

* * *

Someone had been killed on the edge of the camp, his cattle stolen, and his wife was missing. The news spread the next morning like a flash flood.

Mothers kept their children within sight and no one ventured from the protection of the camp. People scanned the horizon, their eyes full of fear. Who wanted to harm them? Where were they now?

In the afternoon, Moses' and Aaron's messengers came through the camp. "We have been attacked by Amalekites," they said. "Do not go outside the camp without protection. Moses has commanded that all able-bodied men from twenty-one to forty-five years are to gather where he judges the people. Bring your swords, shields, and any other battle supplies you have."

"Amalekites! They're the most barbaric of the desert dwellers," someone said.

"They fight on camels," said someone else.

"And have you seen their swords? Blades as wide as a man's hand," said another.

"Cowards too, always taking advantage of the weak and slow."

Noemi was distressed. Uri was forty-three.

Bezalel wanted to fight despite the fact he wasn't yet twenty-one, but his mother wouldn't hear of it. "It's enough that one of my men must put himself in harm's way."

Hur and Bezalel accompanied Uri to the warrior's meeting. Moses had put his young assistant Joshua in charge of the men. Joshua organized them in groups of two hundred. Men who had brought extra pieces of armor gave it to those who had little or none. Others carried axes, swords of various lengths and shapes, and even some javelins. No one had been in battle for as long as they could remember, and many had to be shown how to put on protection and use a sword. Bezalel cringed as he watched their awkward practice lunges and jabs. This battle was bound to turn out badly.

"Be on your guard throughout the night," said Joshua. "Meet here tomorrow morning at sunrise. While we fight, Moses will stand at the top of the hill with the staff of God in his hand. In this way, we will gain a victory over the Amalekites."

The atmosphere in the camp was tense as the men returned to their tents and told those waiting about the plans. Noemi took special pains to serve manna prepared in Uri's favorite way. The family ate their meal without much conversation as they awaited the morning.

The next day, Uri was up before dawn.

Bezalel awoke when he heard him moving about. "I'll take care of the animals," he said. He dressed and went to the place where their sheep and goat were tethered. He watered them and moved their stakes. As he walked back, he saw men on the move to the meeting place with Joshua.

At their tent, Uri had already left. "I cannot stay here," said Hur. "I'm going to find Moses and watch the battle with him."

"I'll come with you," said Bezalel.

When Bezalel and Hur arrived at the place where the army was to assemble, they found the men ready to set out. Moses and Aaron were there too.

Moses caught sight of Hur and waved him over. "Would you join us on the hill overlooking the battle?"

"I certainly will," said Hur.

Bezalel walked with Aaron, Hur, and Moses as they followed the army out of the camp, across a vast plain. He saw, on the edge of it, another encampment. It had to be the Amalekites.

While the army carried on toward the enemy, Moses led them away from the plain. In silence, they climbed a series of low hills until they came to a vantage point. Looking down, Bezalel saw the two fighting forces now advancing toward each other.

The Amalekites looked fierce and ready, carrying their own assortment of swords, daggers, axes, and bows. Many were on camels while others advanced on foot. Seen from above, their spears formed a pattern of vicious points above their heads.

The Israelites, on the other hand, looked ill-prepared and disorganized. Or did they just appear that way to Bezalel because he knew of their fear and lack of experience? He thought about how his father had strapped on a borrowed bronze shield after the evening meal the day before. Then he had taken up the antique sword that had once belonged to Hur's father and made a few practice thrusts at a pretend enemy. If the other soldiers were as unskilled as Uri, they would need a miracle to come out of this battle victorious. Bezalel breathed a prayer for his father.

As the two forces launched their first attacks, Moses took a stand directly over the battlefield and raised his staff. That motion seemed to inject the Hebrew men with energy. Their movements changed from timid and clumsy to purposeful and effective. Soon they had forced the Amalekites some distance back, though the enemy had by no means given up and fought against the Israeli fighters in hand-to-hand combat.

But the Hebrew advantage was unquestionable. Bezalel could hardly believe his eyes. "We're winning!" he exclaimed.

Just as suddenly, the direction of the fight changed as the Amalekites surged forward and the Israelites were forced back. What had happened? Bezalel glanced over at Moses. He had lowered his staff and looked pale and unwell.

"Look at Moses!" he said to Hur. "He needs help."

Hur, who had been intent on watching the battle, now went over to Moses. Aaron also rushed to his side. As Hur supported Moses, he looked around and, motioning with his chin toward a large flat rock a short distance away, called to Bezalel, "Get that stone. Roll it over here so Moses has a seat."

Bezalel ran to the rock. With all his strength, he wrenched it from its place and rolled it the few yards toward Moses until it was directly behind him. Aaron and Hur lowered Moses onto it.

"That feels better," said Moses.

While all this was happening, Bezalel remained vaguely aware of the battle below. He sensed that it wasn't going well for the Israelites. As he looked down again, he saw that the Amalekites had pushed them back a great distance. In fact, some Israeli soldiers had broken from their ranks and were running toward home.

"The battle!" said Moses. "I must raise my staff for the battle." Again he held his staff high. The change below was instantaneous and remarkable. The Israeli warriors turned with purpose and energy to fight off the Amalekites, who shortly began retreating again.

Moses held his staff steady for a long time, but then it began to quiver and he lowered it again. "My arm," he said. "I can't keep holding it up."

The results when Moses lowered his arm were as immediate and negative as they had been positive when he'd raised it. It was clear that as long as Moses' staff was raised over the battlefield, the Israelites were successful. As soon as he lowered it, the Amalekites gained the upper hand.

"We must help him," said Hur, lifting Moses' hand.

The battle went on all day. Between Aaron and Hur, they kept Moses' hand steady and the staff raised over the battlefield. Under the hot sun, Bezalel watched and gave the three men sips of water from the water skin he carried.

By sundown, the Amalekites had had enough. Many of them lay dead on the ground, and the ones who remained turned and fled into the desert.

Joshua led an exuberant army back to camp while Aaron, Hur, and Bezalel helped an exhausted Moses down the hill and back toward the camp.

Bezalel went to sleep that night with scenes of battle playing in his head. He could still hardly believe that their motley army had defeated the Amalekites. Yahweh had helped them again. He had transformed a crowd of inexperienced slaves into victorious warriors. He had honored their ineffectual efforts with victory. This was the Yahweh to which he had pledged his life. How could he ever doubt Him again?

It wasn't until the next morning that Bezalel realized he had promised to meet Sebia the day before to deliver her mother's necklace.

CHAPTER

twenty-two

BEZALEL WAS DELAYED IN DELIVERING HIS PROJECT TO SEBIA WHEN Noemi asked him to care for the animals. Uri had received a slight wound in the battle and needed rest to recover. When he was finally ready to join Zamri, he took the linen parcel with Sebia's bracelet from under his bedroll and slipped it into his basket. He ventured out into the sun-warmed morning air and jogged through the camp to the outskirts where the manna lay.

He glanced over the manna gatherers, and then saw Zamri—and Sebia. She was working next to his sister.

"Shalom," he said as he reached them.

"Shalom," said Sebia. "I was worried about you. Until I talked to Zamri. She told me you weren't in the army yesterday but watched the battle with Moses."

"Yes," said Bezalel, "it was quite the sight." He looked over at Zamri, who was watching the two of them. Her scrutiny made Bezalel self-conscious. Did she think there was anything between them? "Sebia asked me to make a bracelet for her mother."

"Oh," said Zamri.

"And here it is," he said, handing Sebia the package right in front of Zamri, as if he needed to prove his point.

While Zamri watched, Sebia pulled at the end of the cord, loosened the bow that secured the parcel, opened the knot, and unfolded the linen that held the trinket. In the light, both girls admired the elegant gold almond blossoms linked together with perfectly shaped gold circlets.

"She will love this!" said Sebia. "Thank you!" She gave Bezalel such a radiant smile that he was sure his face betrayed his feelings.

Sebia wrapped the bracelet securely in the cloth again. Then she fished a packet of her own from one of her baskets. "I hope this is payment enough."

"I'm sure it will be," Bezalel said, not bothering to open it.

Side-by-side, the three of them collected manna until Zamri's basket was full.

Zamri got to her feet. "I'm going," she said. "We'll have enough when you fill yours." She motioned toward Bezalel's container, which was already half full.

"Yes," said Bezalel. "I'll be back shortly." He was eager to be alone with Sebia again, though they were in the company of hundreds of others.

"The battle yesterday was amazing," he said now, breaking the silence.

"That's what I heard. My father fought. He said it went back and forth and the outcome was never entirely certain. It had something to do with Moses watching from the hilltop."

"That was the miraculous thing," said Bezalel. He told her about how he had seen the tide of battle change, depending on whether or not Moses held his staff above the battlefield.

"Yahweh is truly incredible," said Sebia. "But with His great might, I wonder why He doesn't just perform the miracle? Why did my father, yours, and others have to go out to war to get the victory over the Amalekites?"

"I've wondered the same thing," said Bezalel. "He seems to require action on our part to bring His miracles to pass." Even as he said the words, a thought occurred to him. His miracle would be to gain the hand of Sebia as his wife. Perhaps there was something he could do to make it happen.

They worked on in silence until both their baskets were full. Together, they walked back toward camp.

"I can hardly wait to give mother the bracelet," Sebia said as they came to the place where their paths separated. "She will be so pleased with it."

And I'd like to give something to you, Bezalel thought as they parted and he walked alone the rest of the way back to the tent. Could he make something beautiful enough to convince Sebia to marry him instead of Ethan?

"What took you so long?" Noemi asked as Bezalel delivered his basket of manna.

"I was talking with a friend," he said.

"And who might that friend be?"

"A girl who asked me to make something for her mother."

"Named Sebia?" asked Noemi.

Zamri must be behind this, he thought, looking around for her. She wasn't there. "Yes," he said, a defensive note in his voice. "I was giving her what I made."

"That's all?" She looked like she didn't believe him.

"Of course," Bezalel said. "What did you think?"

"I don't think it's wise for you to spend time with her."

"Why?"

"For one thing, she's betrothed to someone else."

"No, she isn't. She told me she hasn't agreed to the arrangement."

"Well, that's a surprise. It's not what I heard," said Noemi. "But other stories about her are going around too."

"What stories?"

"I don't want to repeat them. Perhaps they are rumors. You know how things can get blown up. I'm just warning you not to get involved."

"She is the most beautiful, honest person I've ever met," said Bezalel. "What people are saying—don't believe them. They're lies. I'm sure of it."

Noemi was quiet for a minute. Then she put her face close to his, like she had when he was a little boy, and looked straight into his eyes. "Bezalel, please. Listen to me. Don't entangle yourself with her."

* * *

With his bracelet for Sebia's mother delivered, and disturbed by his mother's words, Bezalel decided to spend the day away from his work. He went to visit Oholiab.

"What have you been doing with yourself?" asked Oholiab as Saria set tea and a special treat of dried figs in front of them. "Did you fight against the Amalekites? I heard about it late and offered my help, but they had no armor to fit me."

"No, I'm too young," replied Bezalel. "But I spent the day with my grandfather. He helped hold up Moses' arms as our army defeated the Amalekites. I was on the hill, watching the battle with them."

"Tell me about the battle," said Oholiab, leaning forward with interest.

As Bezalel described what he had seen, Oholiab listened in open-mouthed amazement. "Yahweh truly is amazing," he said as Bezalel came to the end of the story.

"Now it's back to the jewelry jobs that keep coming in," Bezalel went on. "Remember the piece I made for Saria? Since that project, many of us craftsmen work together at a place on the edge of the camp. I just made a bracelet in an almond flower design. It turned out nicely."

"For once not an edible," said Oholiab with a twinkle in his eye. "It's a good thing I work with fabrics and not wood or gold." He bit into his fifth fig while Bezalel finished his first.

Bezalel had planned to tell Oholiab about Sebia and his mother's warning, but now he decided against it. He didn't need someone else warning him against her.

"And you?" he asked Oholiab. "What have you been doing?"

"There are always orders for fabrics," Oholiab replied. "Everyone needs clothes. Though I've noticed that what we brought out from Egypt, of both shoes and clothing, has stood up remarkably well despite the conditions. My last project was a robe for Saria. Saria!" He turned, calling to his wife, who was behind a partition in another part of the tent. "Show Bezalel the robe I just finished."

A few minutes later, Saria came out wearing an Egyptian garment that had been altered to an Israeli style. What had once been a tight-fitting Egyptian dress was now a flowing robe. The pleated white linen was embroidered with colorful threads in patterns of birds, fish, and plants, though Bezalel noted bare sections with a myriad of tiny holes where it looked like the embroidery had been picked out.

"You've done an amazing job," Bezalel said as Saria turned slowly to let them see the garment from every angle.

"I took out some of the decorations," Oholiab said. "There were likenesses of the Egyptian gods and writing. I didn't want their images in my house, and as for the writing… well, I just didn't know what it said."

"That must have been a lot of work."

"It was, but I think worth it. When I look back on my time in Egypt, I remember it as oppressive and dark. Despite the bright sun, there was a heaviness in the land. I didn't want to keep any of that darkness."

"Now that you mention it, I agree," said Bezalel. "I once wore an Egyptian charm myself. Only after I took it off did my spirit feel lighter."

"Yes, lighter in spirit," said Oholiab. "Perfectly said. I feel a new freedom and creativity in my work here, even though the conditions are harsh." His eyes twinkled as he patted his rounded stomach.

Bezalel grinned. "Looks like the manna agrees with you."

Little Obed ran by and Bezalel pretended to lunge at the boy. He put on an extra burst of speed to get to his father and jumped into Oholiab's lap. When Bezalel kept looking at him, he put his hands in front of his face as if shy, but he peered at Bezalel through splayed fingers.

"I'll get you," said Bezalel.

He laughed, stood up, and made as if to pounce on the little boy. Obed held his hands over his stomach as Bezalel reached to tickle him, giggling as he pressed tighter to his father.

"Yes, Yahweh is good!" said Oholiab. "When I work and watch the colored threads come together to make a pattern, all the threads fitting tightly to make a piece of new cloth, I see the picture of how Yahweh weaves us. I love His daily provision. I think often about His rescue from impossible situations and the help that always comes just in time. I wish I had some way of expressing my thanks. If only He wore clothes, I would make Him the most beautiful garments of all."

"And I could make the jewelry," said Bezalel, getting caught up in Oholiab's fantasy. "A crown like the Pharaoh wore, and a silver collar studded with amethysts, emeralds, carnelian, and topaz, gold finger rings, earrings, arm bands, belts… our Yahweh would shine like the sun."

Bezalel lost track of time and forgot about his dilemma over Sebia as he spent the day with Oholiab, Saria, and Obed. How wonderful it was to be with someone who understood him while at the same time challenging him to serve Yahweh.

He returned to his tent that night determined to please Yahweh with the skill of his hands. And wouldn't it be wonderful, he reflected as he lay down on his mat, to use that skill with Sebia at his side, like Oholiab had Saria? For he wanted her, no matter what lies people were spreading.

twenty-three

BEZALEL PAID LITTLE ATTENTION TO THE CAVALCADE OF CAMELS THAT made their slow way along the desert road just beyond the manna fields the next morning. He was more interested in whether Sebia would come out. Hopefully he would have a few minutes with her. He'd been pondering what design he should choose for her gift and hoped to gather some clues about what she liked.

She never came, so he wasn't sure what design to cast for the matched necklace and earrings he had decided to make for her, a gift he hoped would win her love. It was a hope that had only grown stronger during yesterday's visit with Oholiab and Saria.

Later, when the family had their morning meal and Hur expressed a desire to again observe Moses judge the people, Bezalel decided to spend a few hours watching that before continuing with his projects.

They got to the place where Moses customarily sat in judgment to find that many had assembled but Moses was nowhere in sight. However, there were camels tethered outside his tent.

The people who were waiting to present their cases to Moses had formed a long line and the onlookers grew ever more restless. Someone was about to go to Moses' tent to investigate the delay when Aaron appeared.

"Shalom, men and women of Israel. I'm so sorry you've had to wait. Moses should be out soon. Visitors have come. But as I said, he should be out soon. Don't be angry or upset."

He ducked back into the tent while the people continued to wait and wait. Finally, almost an hour later, Moses emerged. On one side of him was an elderly black man with wiry white hair and beard, dressed in the fine clothes of a desert prince. On the other side stood a tall woman wearing a colorful woven dress with matching turban. Bezalel's eyes were dazzled by the gold in her ears and the intricate necklace that glittered against her mahogany neck.

In front of Moses stood two boys—around his own age, Bezalel thought. They had lighter skin than the man and woman, but the same kinky hair as the man, only darkest black.

"Men and women of Israel," Moses said. "Today is a joyous day for me. For today my father-in-law Jethro has come. Please welcome him."

The people bowed and a murmured "Shalom, shalom" swept through the crowd.

Moses went on. "He has also brought my wife Zipporah." He put his arm around the woman's shoulder momentarily, then removed it to place his hands on the heads of the two boys. "These are my sons, Gershom and Eliezer."

Bezalel was surprised. He'd had no idea Moses was married—let alone had children. He wondered what it would be like to have Moses as a father. Somehow the leader didn't seem like a fatherly sort.

"I know you will understand that we must cancel the judgment today. But I will be here to judge tomorrow."

Bezalel wondered if it was just his imagination, but did Moses seem softer and kinder today? Meanwhile, Aaron circulated among the people. Bezalel overheard him calming those who were annoyed by the change of plans.

"I'm sorry you've been inconvenienced. So sorry. Come back tomorrow and we'll make sure you get a hearing."

How different the two brothers were.

* * *

Later that day, a messenger came to extend an invitation to Hur. "As one of the elders, you've been invited to meet with Moses and Jethro," he said.

Hur was visibly pleased. He put on his best clothes and hurried away.

It was late evening when he returned. He was in good spirits when he entered the tent. "You all waited up for me?" he asked.

"Tell us everything," said an eager Bezalel.

"What is Jethro like?" asked Noemi. "Did you learn anything about our trip—how long until we reach Canaan, that sort of thing?"

"No," said Hur with a chuckle. "If that's what you were expecting, I'm afraid you will be disappointed. But Jethro is a fine, godly man. He's a priest. First he spoke an eloquent benediction over us. Then he and Moses made a burnt offering and we all ate together. Tomorrow he is going to attend Moses' judging session. I wonder what he'll make of that."

Hur chuckled as if laughing at a private joke.

* * *

The next day, the three men went to the place where Moses judged the people. The queue seemed longer than Bezalel had ever seen it. Even though they'd gotten there earlier than usual, Moses was already hard at work. Jethro sat beside him, watching everything.

"My neighbor's baby never stops crying," said the man who stood before Moses and Jethro. "My whole family can't get any sleep."

Bezalel watched as Moses dealt with that complaint and then faced the next—a woman who accused her neighbor of stealing a basket of manna, and the next—a man who suspected his relative of putting a curse on his wife so she was unable to conceive. And so it went, hour after hour.

Bezalel left when the sun was still high in the sky. He had seen all this before and it was time to get back to work. But when he returned home for the evening meal, his father and grandfather still weren't home.

"Moses was there all day," Hur said when he and Uri finally returned home at sunset. "I'll be surprised if Jethro doesn't have something to say about this. I hope he does. I've thought for a long time that this is too much for Moses."

* * *

The family was still at breakfast the next day when Aaron's courier arrived with a message for Hur. His presence was again requested. He was still gone when Bezalel returned from working all day, so he and Uri went to investigate.

They arrived at the spot where Moses customarily judged the people to find a very different scene. On the ground around Moses sat the leaders of Israel, Hur among them. Moses stood in the center. He was speaking about the decrees and laws that he enforced each day in his judgments, telling stories and giving examples.

Bezalel and Uri sat at a distance and listened until the sun set and the meeting broke up.

"I am now a judge in Israel," Hur said as they made their way home. "Jethro suggested Moses split up the work. We have spent the day in school, learning the job. Now, my son and grandson, you must be especially good, as you are living with a judge."

twenty-four

THAT NIGHT, BEZALEL LOOKED OVER THE GOLD HE HAD RECEIVED AS payment for the things he had made. He had been saving it for the time they would get to Canaan, but now he had another purpose; he wanted to use it for Sebia's gift. He saw that there wasn't nearly enough for the design he had in mind. It was a good thing his work was in demand, he thought as he replaced his collection under his sleeping mat.

He was already hard at work the next morning when the other goldsmiths arrived at the workplace with their projects and tools.

"You're here early," Shoshan said.

"Lots of orders to fill," said Bezalel.

"Is Bezalel here?" asked someone who came by shortly after. Judging from the parcel under his arm, he wanted work done.

"I am," Bezalel replied.

"I need a special ring made, within the next few days if possible."

"I'll do it for you," Bezalel said. As they discussed design and payment, another man arrived. Shoshan talked to him, but when Bezalel overheard Shoshan turn down the job, he jumped in. "I'll do it."

People kept coming with requests, and he had just returned to his workstation after accepting three more assignments when Abnosh approached him. "You don't have to take all the work, you know," Abnosh said. "We're all capable of making these things."

"I know," said Bezalel. "But they often ask for me and I need—"

"They would ask for others if you gave us a chance," said Abnosh.

"You're not as talented as you think you are," Bezalel heard one of Abnosh's friends mutter.

"Only conceited and greedy," said another under his breath.

For the rest of the day, the words of his fellow craftsmen troubled Bezalel.

"Why so quiet tonight?" asked Grandpa Hur that night after the evening meal. "Is something troubling you?"

"It's something a colleague at the workplace said today," said Bezalel. "I was taking orders when some of the others called me conceited and greedy for taking jobs for myself and not offering them to others."

"And were you doing that?" asked Grandpa Hur.

"Well, in a way."

"Why?"

"The people ask for me," said Bezalel. "And the gold I earn will help me get established in my own shop once we get to Canaan." Of course, he couldn't tell his grandfather that right now he needed to collect gold for another reason.

"Saving for a shop is an honorable thing," said Hur. "And you do have an extraordinary gift. I can understand why people would come to you. But don't let their attention or praise swell your head. Who created you with your talent in the first place?"

"God did," said Bezalel.

"Yes," said Hur. "And He gives these special gifts for a purpose. Ever since you were little, I've had the conviction that your talent was no accident. I believe Yahweh has a special purpose for it, something bigger than serving Egypt's gods, making trinkets, or even starting your own shop in Canaan. Only beware that you don't get sidetracked with ambition, pride, or the desire for wealth."

Bezalel was surprised at his grandfather's words—and a little hurt. He had expected sympathy, not a lecture. Still, Grandpa Hur had said some things that made him think. His mention of praise made Bezalel think back to Egypt and how important hearing the praise of his overseers had been to him. Things hadn't changed. He still loved to hear compliments on his work.

Grandpa Hur sounded a lot like Oholiab, whose dream was to serve Yahweh with his talent with fabrics. But how could that be more than a dream? Yahweh didn't have a shape like the gods of Egypt. How could one ever use gold and cloth to honor an invisible God?

* * *

"We've heard you do wonderful gold work, and I see it's true," said the man, motioning to the piece Bezalel was currently forming. He and the woman beside him were well dressed in the Egyptian style.

Several weeks had passed and Bezalel had begun working on Sebia's gift. Between other jobs, he had cast and polished the pieces of the necklace and earrings he had designed.

Since the blowup with Abnosh, he had been careful to defer to other craftsmen, even when customers requested him for jobs. Still, there was an undercurrent of discontent amongst the workmen that troubled him.

"We have a collection of things we got from the Egyptians," the man continued. He opened the bundle he was carrying to reveal a rich pile of collars, arm and leg bands, amulets, pendants, and rings. "Our request is a little different than what you usually do. Less work for you." He chuckled, though Bezalel thought he detected a note of embarrassment in his laugh. "We'd like you to simply link each emblem to form one golden collar."

"Cast into what shapes?" asked Bezalel.

"Not recast," said the man. "We want to preserve the Egyptian magic that is present in each piece."

"You want to go around the camp of Israel wearing a collar of Egyptian charms?" Bezalel's voice reflected his surprise.

The woman, who had been silent until now, spoke up. "We wouldn't wear it around the camp. We would be content with that power in our tent."

As he grasped their intention, Bezalel's surprise turned to chagrin. "Never!" he said. "What gives you the idea that I would tempt Yahweh like this?"

"Well… we just thought…" the man began.

"Please leave and take your Egyptian charms and amulets with you." Bezalel's voice was quiet but firm. "I would never aid you in your plans for secret sorcery. I cannot do this."

"Oh, but I can!" Abnosh had come over to where Bezalel and the couple spoke.

"That's not a good idea, Abnosh," Bezalel said. "Why would you tempt God? Have you forgotten that Yahweh defeated the Egyptian gods? Have you forgotten the plagues?"

"What does that have to do with me?" Abnosh fired back. "You have no right to refuse this project or order these fine folks to leave on anyone's behalf but your own. You just want to keep us from earning a little something for ourselves." Turning to the couple, he went on, "I am more than willing to help you."

All the workers had stopped to listen to the exchange. There was a smattering of applause as Abnosh led the two to his workstation to get their further instructions while Bezalel resumed his work in stunned silence. How had things come to this?

* * *

At last, the day came when Sebia's gift was ready. He held up the necklace of linked hexagons. The gold pieces winked and glowed in the late afternoon light. It was beautiful. He wrapped the pieces in linen, as he had the gift for her mother, and when he got home he hid it under his sleeping mat.

He had avoided going out to gather manna for all the time he was at work on Sebia's gift because he was afraid of meeting her. He had feared he would give away his surprise, but most afraid, if he was perfectly honest, that she would tell him she had decided to say yes to Ethan and was formally betrothed. Somehow he couldn't face the possibility that their friendship could be over.

The next morning, he awoke before the sun was even up. He lay on his mat, his mind going over the scenario of meeting Sebia again and finally giving her the gift. He imagined her face, lit up the way it had looked when he'd given her the bracelet for her mother. He never went past that, though, because he wasn't sure what he expected or could hope would happen next. He couldn't simply ask her to marry him. That just wasn't how things were done, especially since his parents didn't approve of her.

Finally he heard Hur stirring, then Uri. He got dressed himself and peeked behind the partition where Zamri slept. She was still fast asleep, so he went over to Noemi, who had yawned and stretched awake.

"I'll gather manna today," he said. "Let Zamri sleep."

He took the parcel from under his mat and tied it around his waist with his girdle. He took his family's manna baskets and went out into the frigid desert air.

The place outside the camp where they collected manna was still deserted. What was he thinking, going out so early? If she came at all, Sebia usually came out late, not early. Oh well, he'd just work slowly, stretching out the job until she arrived. And if she didn't come out today, he'd come again tomorrow, and the next day.

He dawdled at gathering the sweet, brittle flakes. As more and more people came out, he surveyed the land, sure that Sebia would appear at any moment.

The sun beat down on the desert plain, warming the air. He took off the robe that had warmed him in the early morning chill and tied it around his waist, then continued to place manna in his basket, slowly, stacking it in neat rows. When others came to pick beside him, he moved on to more isolated spots. When Sebia did finally come out, he wanted to be alone with her.

Finally, when both baskets were heaped high and the warm sun threatened to melt the manna that still remained on the ground, he saw her in the distance. Despite his better judgment, he waved at her. She looked his way, gave a quick reply wave, and came toward him.

"Shalom," he said when she was within earshot. "You are late today."

"My little brother was supposed to do this," she said, "but he isn't well, so Mother sent me. Looks like you've been here for a while." She looked at his heaping baskets, then into his eyes. As always when she looked at him that way, he lost all good sense.

She was the first to drop her glance, then crouched down and began gathering.

"You can have some of mine," he said, pouring a generous amount from his basket into hers.

"Thank you! How have you been? I haven't seen you for a while."

"Busy," he said. Was this the time? He decided to take a chance that it was. Untying the parcel from his waist, he handed it to her. "I've been making this."

"What?" Her forehead furrowed in puzzlement as she looked up at him.

"Take it," he said, handing it to her. "It's for you."

Her mouth opened with incredulity. "For me? I didn't order another one. I don't have anything to pay you."

"No," said Bezalel. "It's a gift."

She took the parcel and turned it in her hand, testing its heft. Then she undid the twine that held it together and unwrapped the folds of cloth to reveal the glimmering gold trinkets.

"Oh," she murmured. She fingered them, examining the earrings that flashed in the sun, feeling the heavy weight of the necklace.

Bezalel watched closely, trying to gauge her reaction.

At last she looked up and their eyes met. "They're stunning," she said. "But why?"

Bezalel didn't know what to say. This is where he'd come to in his daydreams but gone no further. He looked at her a long time without speaking, then said at last, "I just wanted to."

She looked down, took a deep breath as if gathering courage, then glanced up at him, an apprehensive look in her eye. "I don't know if I can accept them."

Bezalel had never thought of this—that she would like the gift but not accept it. Of course, what a fool he'd been not to consider that possibility.

"You don't want it?" he asked. His voice sounded disappointed.

"It's not that," said Sebia, looking up at him with pleading in her eyes. "It's beautiful, and I love it. It's just that if Ethan finds out I have accepted this from you, he'll be angry."

"Have you accepted his proposal then?"

"No. But my father has his heart set on this marriage. When I told him the other day that I didn't want to be betrothed, he was furious. He's a great fan of Ethan's father and so proud that Dathan wants his son to marry me."

As she talked, Bezalel could see how upset she was and he berated himself for putting her in such a position. He reached out his hand to take the gift back.

"Don't keep it," he said. "I understand."

She held on to the pieces, looking at them, touching the surfaces with her fingers as if trying to memorize them. Finally she looked up at him again, and this time there was recognition and understanding in her eyes.

"You gave me this because you love me, don't you?"

He looked down. "Yes, but I'm a fool to put you in a spot like this. I should have thought it through. I don't know what I imagined would happen."

"I want it as a memory of our friendship," she said quietly. "I won't tell anyone. And I'll pray that Yahweh will work it out."

"So will I," said Bezalel. He dumped more manna from his baskets into hers and then headed back to camp, leaving her to finish her gathering alone.

When his mother asked him to go out and gather manna the next morning, Bezalel didn't really want to go, but he did anyway. He made quick work of it this time, never looking up once to see if Sebia was around. As much as he had anticipated meeting her yesterday, he dreaded seeing her today, fearful to find that her gift had caused her trouble or that she had changed her mind and decided to return it after all.

The thought of working at his projects also lost its allure. Now that Sebia's gift was completed, the pull of the workplace wasn't nearly as strong as it had been.

Still, he had projects to finish, and many of the less experienced goldsmiths depended on him for instruction and help. After the morning meal, he took his tools and materials and went again to the work area at the edge of camp.

As he melted, formed, hammered, and polished, he again mulled over what Hur had said the night after his first clash with Abnosh. Did Yahweh really have a larger purpose for his talent than this? Now that he had completed his gift for Sebia, he had to face the fact that his other projects didn't inspire him in the same way. Could he spend the rest of his life making trinkets? But what else would he do?

In Egypt, there had been new things to learn, different techniques to try, a whole religious system that needed fine things made of gold. But Yahweh was not such a God. He didn't need any gold or craftsmen. How could Grandpa say with such confidence that Yahweh had a special purpose for his talent? If there was such a purpose, it certainly wasn't obvious.

He was deep in contemplation and didn't notice someone standing over him until a sharp voice cut into his thoughts.

"Hey, you. Are you Bezalel?"

Bezalel looked up to see a heavyset man peering down at him. There was cold anger in his eyes. He pulled a parcel from the folds of his robe and threw it at Bezalel's feet. It was the package he had given Sebia yesterday.

"How dare you give this gift to my betrothed!" he growled.

Bezalel was stunned. His first impulse was to cower under the man's rage. But another part of him rose up at Ethan's presumption, and he heard himself reply, "She's not your betrothed."

"Who told you that?" Ethan asked, outrage all over his face.

"Sebia herself," Bezalel answered. He realized a moment later that with that answer, he may just have sprung the trap that had been set for him.

Ethan's face grew red and his eyes looked as if they would pop from their sockets. "You have spent time with her?"

"Only out in the desert, picking manna where everyone could see us," said Bezalel. "Never in secret."

"You think I believe that?" Ethan gave the parcel a kick. "Don't you ever go near her again—anywhere! And wait for a summons to Moses' court. I will be bringing a complaint against you at the next opportunity. No one gets away with defiling my woman!"

"She's not your woman," said Bezalel, now thoroughly roused. "You don't own her."

Ethan glared at Bezalel, then lunged at him, grabbing him by the shoulders and twisting him to the ground. They wrestled, writhing and squirming and grunting, first one and then the other gaining the upper hand. But Bezalel was no match for the stocky Ethan. Ethan soon had him pinned beneath his beefy body. Holding him down, he reached for Bezalel's right hand. Forcing it flat onto the ground, Ethan raised himself on hands and knees, then brought his left knee down on it with all his might.

"That'll teach you," he growled.

Bezalel heard a crunch, felt searing pain, and then everything went black.

He regained consciousness to see Shoshan trying to rouse him by pouring water on his face. He tried to sit up, but the movement made him feel sick and he had to lie down again.

"Where's Ethan?" he asked, hardly able to get the words out.

"He left," said Shoshan. "Here, let's look at your hand."

When Shoshan moved it, the jolt of pain made Bezalel gasp.

"It looks bad." Shoshan grimaced. "It's misshapen and starting to swell. Bones are probably broken."

"Can you gather my tools?" asked Bezalel a few hours later when he felt steady enough to walk home. "And put in that parcel."

He motioned to the package that Ethan had returned, then watched as Shoshan tied his tools into the folds of the familiar old robe. Would he ever use them again?

PART FOUR

Outcast

twenty-five CHAPTER

"What happened to you?" Noemi asked as Bezalel entered the tent. His injury was obvious, for Shoshan had wrapped his hand in a sling to ease the pain when he walked.

"Here are your tools," Shoshan said, handing Bezalel the parcel he had carried for him.

"Thank you, friend," said Bezalel as Shoshan left for his own tent.

"What happened?" asked Noemi again.

"A disagreement at work. It's not much. I'll be fine."

"Let me look at it."

Bezalel winced as she examined his hand, now reddish purple and twice its normal size. "It looks like some bones are broken. We'll need to have it set so it mends properly," she said. She sent Uri for a physician, who inflicted the most excruciating pain Bezalel had ever felt as he eased the broken bones into place, then bound the hand between splints.

"Whatever caused someone to do this to you?" asked Noemi.

"I don't want to talk about it."

That night, before going to sleep, Bezalel clumsily untied the robe that held his tools. He took out Sebia's parcel, undid it, and looked inside. There were the earrings, just as he had made them, though the necklace had been wrenched in two.

The pounding pain in his hand kept him awake and he wrestled with his thoughts. What had he set in motion by making that gift for Sebia? Had Ethan come after her too? Surely the broken necklace meant some sort of violent encounter. And what next? If Ethan hauled him in front of Moses and the judges—his own grandfather now one of them—how would he defend himself?

He hoped, above all, that Sebia's reputation wouldn't be tarnished. He couldn't bear the thought that by giving her that impulsive gift he had called into question her innocence and purity.

Finally, sleep came. He awoke the next morning to the sound of hustle and bustle.

"You're awake at least!" exclaimed Noemi. "I know you've had a bad night, and I didn't want to wake you, but now that you're up, it's time to get moving. The cloud has lifted and we're getting packed."

Bezalel's first feeling was relief. At least Ethan wouldn't haul him before Moses' tribunal today. Though walking for miles with his injured hand wouldn't be easy.

As usual, the order to break camp was sudden and hurried. The people had few possessions and getting packed up was a matter of an hour or two.

For Bezalel, packing took twice as long as usual, and for some things he had to ask for help. Soon the tent was down and all their clothes and household belongings bound in parcels that they strapped to the donkey or onto their own backs. Bezalel felt the weight of his tools.

Maybe I should leave them behind. They only got me into trouble. But no, he couldn't do that. He slung them onto his back and carried them in the usual way.

As they took their place in the multitude, Bezalel looked back at Rephidim. He couldn't believe that the empty plain had housed their thousands. So much had happened there in the last few weeks. He was glad to be gone from the place with its bad memories. If only he could go back and undo the events of the past few days. What he wouldn't do to replace his current pain and the weight of worry with the carefree existence he'd had when they first arrived.

* * *

The walk through the desert always exacted a toll of weariness on the people. Their brisk morning pace soon slowed as families stopped to eat, drink, and tend their animals. Often during midday, when the sun was hottest, the whole multitude halted. Families put up temporary canopies to shelter themselves from the sun, eat a little food, and rest or nap in preparation for the cooler hours ahead when they resumed their travels.

They traveled like this for several days through the desert of Sinai. With the passage of time, Bezalel's worry eased a little. No doubt Ethan had confronted Bezalel when his temper was at its hottest. By now he would have had some time to cool down. Hopefully he would rethink his threat to bring Bezalel before the judges. Surely he would realize that such a case would not only reflect badly on Bezalel but also on Sebia, his future wife.

Then, one day, the cloud stopped near a mountain. People said it was Mount Sinai. Word circulated that this was where Moses had first met God at the burning bush. Someone pointed out that it was the beginning of the month of Sivan, exactly three months since they had left Egypt. What would their stay at this place bring, Bezalel wondered?

* * *

After their camp was set up, Bezalel didn't know what to do with himself. He was accustomed to being busy, but now he couldn't move his fingers without exquisite pain. Even when he was still, his hand ached and throbbed. What if the damage to his hand was permanent? What if he could never work again? He couldn't imagine life without doing the job that had been part of him for as long as he could remember.

He thought back to his time in Egypt, when he hadn't given a thought to whether or not he worked or why. There, of course, he hadn't had any choice; he worked whether he felt like it or not. But underlying that work had been a sense of purpose. He had been providing something that his Egyptian masters needed and appreciated. He remembered them now.

Rahotep had first seen his talent and set him up to work in the shop of Suty the carver. When Suty's jealous son Sutymose had betrayed him and he lost Suty's favor, Rahotep had sent him to work with Khafra. But over the years, he had also been sent to do projects for others—Nesmut the perfumer and Hori the gem cutter. In each case, he had labored more for their praise than for anything else, not fully grasping that his work was being used to serve the Pharaoh, Ra, and the multitude of Egyptian deities that Yahweh opposed.

Of course, Moses' coming had enlightened him. With his plagues, he had shown them that Yahweh was the God with power—the one to serve. And so here he was, not only away from where his talents were needed for important things, but, because of his own foolishness, stopped from working altogether.

If only he could believe that Yahweh had a reason for making him the way he was, like Grandpa Hur said. He felt all wrong—like a misfit, a big mistake. It was a feeling only made worse by his broken hand.

He needed to talk to someone who would understand. He would go to see Oholiab.

* * *

Bezalel caught Oholiab and Saria relaxing with some tea and manna after getting settled in their camp. Their tent, with its brightly-dyed mats and colorful partitions, always cheered him. Oholiab didn't believe only in making things for others, but also in surrounding himself with the work of his hands.

It must be an effective advertisement for his services, Bezalel thought.

As usual, Oholiab was delighted to see him, but dismayed at his injured hand. "What happened?" he asked.

Bezalel told him everything. "And now I'm stopped from working, I don't know if I'll ever be able to work again, and I'll probably soon be busy defending myself before Moses and the other judges. One is my grandfather. How humiliating for both him and me!"

"But you've done nothing wrong," said Oholiab. "Sebia told you she wasn't betrothed, so you weren't violating any law. And if, as you say, you only ever met out in the open, you can't be charged with anything."

"Perhaps I shouldn't worry," said Bezalel. "But it's Sebia's and my word against Ethan's, which means she'll probably be dragged into this. It's all my fault. In some ways I feel like my broken hand is punishment for what I've done. Perhaps it's a sign that Yahweh is displeased with me. Perhaps it means I'm doing the wrong thing and that I shouldn't pursue my craft anymore. But what else could I do? My work is who I am."

"I wouldn't read too much into your broken hand," said Oholiab. "Look at all the setbacks Moses had when he was freeing us from Egypt. Even after we left, it looked like the Egyptians would bring us back. But in the middle of the biggest trouble of all, Yahweh opened up the Red Sea and we escaped the Egyptians for good."

"So you think my broken hand is just a temporary setback?" asked Bezalel. "Do you think I might work again?"

"I do," said Oholiab. "Your gift is rare and unusual, and I'm sure Yahweh gave it to you for a reason. Look at your broken hand as a test. Someday perhaps you'll understand Yahweh's plan in even this thing that seems like a problem now."

"That reminds me of something I heard Moses say back in Egypt," said Bezalel. "One night he ate with us. When my grandfather asked him why our deliverance was taking so long, he said that Yahweh had hardened Pharaoh's heart not only to convince the Egyptians of His power but to help us Hebrews believe in Him too."

"Exactly," said Oholiab. "We trust Yahweh to help us through the tests that come. When we see His help, we trust Him more than ever. As for understanding why these things happen, especially when we're in the middle of them, I like what I once heard a wise man say: 'We live our lives forward, but we understand them backward.'"

Though Bezalel hadn't noticed Saria leave the area of the tent where they were sitting, she reentered now with Obed in her arms. The boy rubbed his eyes, looking like he had just woken from a nap. When he saw Oholiab, he wriggled away from his mother and dashed into his father's arms.

Bezalel watched with a smile as the little boy cuddled with his father, then asked for a bite of the manna Oholiab was putting in his mouth. The homey scene reminded him of how just a short time ago he had dreamed of Sebia and himself in just such a setting. In the last week, he had all but forsaken that dream. But what Oholiab had said reignited it with a spark of hope. Maybe Yahweh was testing him in regard to Sebia as well.

THE NEXT DAY, ONE OF AARON'S COURIERS CAME THROUGH THE CAMP. He stopped at the family's tent and asked to speak with Hur. "Moses has requested a meeting of the elders," he said. "The others may come too, but the elders must come."

Bezalel felt a grip of panic. Could Moses be assembling the elders to hear Ethan's complaint? But surely he wouldn't call for all the leaders to come and hear such a thing.

All the family, even Zamri and her friends, who often spent time at the tent with her, made the twenty-minute walk to the front of the camp. Hur joined the elders, assembled at the front of the congregation, while the rest of the people sat on the ground behind them. Bezalel was relieved to see this was no customary judging session.

Seated with his family in the multitude, Bezalel studied Mount Sinai in front of them. The barren rock rose high into the sky, but its top wasn't visible, for the cloud obscured it. Funny how one got used to something like that cloud and all but ignored it. Seeing it today, directly in front of him, Bezalel studied it, noticing how its roiling depths glowed with light even in the blaze of the sun.

Did Yahweh live within it? What did He look like? Did He even have a shape? Somehow Bezalel couldn't imagine a shapeless being, but neither could he imagine Yahweh in the shape of an animal, bird, or water creature as the Egyptians portrayed their gods.

His thoughts were interrupted as Moses began. The leader spoke on his own this time, without Aaron's assistance.

"Today I met with Yahweh," he began. "This is what He says to you, His people: 'You yourselves have seen what I did to Egypt, and how I carried you on eagles' wings and brought you to Myself. Now if you obey Me fully and keep My covenant, then out of all nations you will be My treasured possession. Although the whole earth is Mine, you will be for Me a kingdom of priests and a holy nation.' Furthermore, Yahweh wants your response to His words to you. What do you as a people say?"

The crowd, which had been perfectly still, started buzzing. Around him, Bezalel heard people discussing the words Moses had spoken. "Maybe the best is still ahead… a treasured possession among the nations… a kingdom of priests. Yes, we'd like to be part of that."

The elders who had sat in the front during Moses' speech now circulated among the people. "What is your answer?" they asked. "Shall we answer yes?"

A chorus of "Yes!" rose throughout crowd.

"So our answer will be, 'We will do everything the Lord has said.'"

The people answered, shouting out in unison, "We will do everything the Lord has said."

Moses heard the words and a rare smile lit his face. Then, even as the people watched, he made his way up the mountain, and the cloud that had hovered over the mountaintop moved down Mount Sinai toward him. Finally he was engulfed in it, no longer visible.

Bezalel felt a shiver as rumbles came from the cloud. He heard Moses speaking faintly. From a distance, their leader was answered by a thunderous voice, though Bezalel couldn't understand its words.

People all around were shocked and dumbfounded at what they were seeing and hearing.

"It's Yahweh!" one whispered. "He's speaking with Moses."

"Who knew that Yahweh spoke directly with him?" asked someone else.

"I'll listen to him more carefully from now on," said another.

Bezalel wasn't sure how long the conversation lasted, but he felt the impact of the nearness of God to the camp. The worries that had consumed him since his fight with Ethan began to fade. As he sat in the shadow of the cloud, he had the sense that he himself was in the presence of Someone who knew him intimately yet still accepted him. He closed his eyes as feelings of light and love washed over him.

With Moses no longer before them, some of the people got up to go. Noemi, Zamri, and her friends must have been with them, for when Bezalel opened his eyes later—he wasn't sure how much later—they were gone. Uri was still there, though, and many others, including the group of elders Moses had summoned.

He observed the cloud. It seemed to be lifting. Then, from its gauzy fringes, a shape appeared. Moses. He had spoken with God and lived to tell them about it. As he neared the assembly, Bezalel noticed his face. It shone in the late afternoon sun as if dusted with a million golden flecks.

"God has spoken again," Moses said as he reached the front of the assembled crowd. "He will show Himself to you. Prepare yourself for His arrival. In three days, He will come. This is what you must do to get ready. Wash your clothes. Refrain from sexual relations. And stay away from the mountain. The word of the Lord is, 'Be careful that you do not go up the mountain or touch the foot of it. Whoever touches the mountain shall surely be put to death. He shall surely be stoned or shot with arrows; not a hand is to be laid on him. Whether man or animal, he shall not be permitted to live.' Only when the ram's horn sounds a long blast may you go up to the mountain."

* * *

Bezalel insisted on regularly gathering the family's manna, even though with one hand it took him far longer than it had before. He did it to feel useful.

The next morning, Noemi was already up and moving around the tent, collecting everyone's clothes in preparation for washing them. Bezalel noticed her troubled face when he handed her his soiled tunic before leaving with the manna baskets. But his heart did a little flip when she said, "Son, I have something to talk to you about when you get back."

Had she heard about his fight with Ethan and Ethan's threat to take him before the judges of Israel? He shuddered at the thought.

Since the day he had given Sebia his gift, he no longer looked for her on the manna fields. In fact, if he did see her, he didn't know what he would do for fear of getting them both into more trouble. But he still thought about her all the time and hoped Ethan hadn't mistreated her.

Bezalel filled his basket as quickly as he could, wondering the whole time what Noemi wanted to discuss. When he returned to the tent, the place was a hubbub of activity with water heating over the fire, clothes soaking in steaming pots, and Noemi and Zamri beside another pot, scrubbing vigorously.

He deposited the basket with manna in the tent and went out to the front of the tent where his mother and Zamri worked. Uri was there too, beckoning Bezalel. "Come, son. We have something to discuss with you."

Noemi, who had looked up when Bezalel arrived, joined them as Uri led the way to the canopy that shaded a spot beside their tent.

Uri sat on the mat that covered the ground and motioned for the others to sit as well. His face was stern, as was Noemi's.

Uri began. "Bezalel, we've heard something about you yesterday that surprised us. We just wanted to hear your side of the story before we do anything about it."

Bezalel looked down. Now he was in for it!

"Rumors are floating around the camp that Dathan will be making a complaint about you before Israel's judges. The complaint is that you have defiled the woman to whom his son is betrothed. What do you say to this?"

Bezalel took a deep breath. He should have known Ethan would twist the story.

"That is not true," he began. "Here's what really happened. I first saw Sebia dancing with Miriam after we crossed the Red Sea. I asked Zamri who she was and Zamri told me she was betrothed. That's why, when I met her, I was very careful to keep my distance. We first talked on the manna plain in the Wilderness of Sin. She asked me to make a bracelet for her mother, which I did. We saw each other from time to time after that. And she told me she *wasn't* betrothed. She said Dathan and her father had discussed her marrying Ethan, but she hadn't said yes."

Bezalel studied his parent's faces as he said this. Did they believe him?

"After I made her mother's bracelet," he continued, "I did a foolish thing. I made a gift for her. I gave it to her one morning while we were gathering manna. That's the only place we have ever met and talked. Out in the open, in full view of everyone. And once or twice, we walked back to the camp together."

"Why did you ever make her such a thing?" his mother asked. "I warned you about her."

"It's not her," said Bezalel. "She did nothing wrong. She wasn't going to accept it. She said she would get in trouble with Ethan and her father, so I told her not to keep it. She started giving it back, but then she changed her mind."

Of course, he couldn't mention to his parents that Sebia had guessed the jewelry was a symbol of his love for her—even though on this bleak morning the memory of that cheered him despite everything.

"Ethan must have found it," Bezalel continued, "because the next day he came to where I was working. He was terribly angry. He returned Sebia's gift and told me never to come near her again. When I said he didn't own her, he attacked me and did this." He lifted his bandaged hand. "And he said he would drag me before the judges."

"This is the truth?" Noemi looked at him with probing eyes. "What you're telling us is exactly what happened?"

"Yes," said Bezalel.

"Well, that's a relief," said Uri. "We heard all kinds of stories. One is that you raped her. Another that you made the gifts for Sebia and her mother as a betrothal price of your own. There are even the rumors circulating about Sebia's behavior in Egypt."

Bezalel put his head in his hands. What had he started with his impetuous gift? He wished he could go back and redo that one thing, if for no other reason than to spare Sebia the pain and humiliation she was going through. Though, if he were really honest, he knew he would change nothing else about their relationship up to that point. He also knew that he felt the same way about Sebia as he ever had. He was sure he would feel the same way no matter what lies people spread about her.

"We will support you, son," said Uri. "It might not be easy, because Dathan is a very vocal man who has a large following. Already he has set many people against you and our family."

Bezalel looked up. "I have been truthful with you. The one I'm really worried about is Sebia. I took her word for it that the betrothal between her and Ethan hadn't been completed. She would never lie. But when Ethan came to me, he insisted she was his betrothed. That means either Sebia or Ethan lied. It will be his word against mine, and you can guess whose word will be trusted, especially if his father uses his influence to get Ethan what he wants. It's ugly."

"You're right. It's ugly and may get uglier," said Uri. "But Yahweh is all for the truth. If you're telling the truth, we must believe that it will ultimately prevail."

twenty-seven

TWO DAYS LATER, THE RUMBLE OF THUNDER WOKE BEZALEL. IT resembled the sound that had come from the mountain a few days before, only much louder. He jumped from his mat, ran to the tent opening, and looked out. There were no clouds anywhere, except on the top of Mount Sinai where the cloud of Yahweh's presence still rested. This morning, it looked ominous and billowed smoke. Even as he watched, another rumble shook the camp. It sent shivers through him.

The others were now awake too, roused by the sound. Bezalel began describing what he had seen when his voice was drowned out by an earsplitting blast. It sounded as if someone had blown a trumpet right beside them.

"What was that?" asked Uri. He went outside to have a look and Bezalel joined him.

All around, people were popping their heads out of tents or standing around, looking worried and frightened. Uri and Bezalel studied the mountain for some time.

"I think this has something to do with the cloud on Mount Sinai," said Bezalel. "See how it's smoking? It looks alive."

Uri looked toward the mountain. "It does," he agreed.

When the men reentered the tent, Noemi was up. "Clean clothes for everyone today, just as Moses commanded," she said as she went to the pile of laundry she had washed, dried, and folded over the last several days. She began to hand out garments to each family member.

Bezalel dressed, then grabbed a manna basket before going out to gather the day's supply. Others were doing the same. The atmosphere was tense as people hurried to get the chore done. Even as he worked, Bezalel heard another rumble from the mountain. He looked up to see a flash of lightning, followed by another deafening thunder crack. Rocks rolled down the mountainside as if some giant animal had run by and dislodged them. His task finally done, he stood, stretched the cramp out of his right arm, stiff from favoring his hand, picked up his basket, and headed for home. Despite himself, he glanced around to see if Sebia was out there somewhere. She wasn't.

When he got back, his family was waiting for him, looking apprehensive though scrubbed and fresh in their clean clothes. Aaron's messenger had come by while he was away to inform them that everyone was to follow Moses to the foot of the mountain.

Noemi took half of the manna from the basket Bezalel had just filled and dumped it into water boiling on the fire. In a few minutes, they were eating the heavy pudding that the manna turned into when cooked. Each then replenished the water they carried in their individual water skins and joined the crowds who were streaming through the camp and onto the plain in front of Mount Sinai.

* * *

The activity on the mountain grew more intense even as they walked through the camp. Someone had made a barricade around the bottom of the mountain using boulders and tent poles. Bezalel wondered who of them besides Moses had shown the courage to go there. He couldn't imagine wanting to be anywhere near that frightening place.

When they got to where the people had gathered, Bezalel stood with his family, looking up at the fearful sight. The cloud shifted and rolled. Smoke billowed from the top as if from a furnace. Lightning continued to flash and the thunder, which had been intermittent, was now a constant rumble. All around him the people watched, speaking in low, worried voices.

Another ear-shattering trumpet blast stilled all conversation.

What was happening? Bezalel's heart galloped and his palms grew sweaty with fear. What was Yahweh going to do, kill them?

In the moment of stillness after the blast, Bezalel heard the skittering of boulders and rocks falling from the slopes in front of them. A minute later, the trumpet sound blared again, louder and louder, until Bezalel put his hands over his ears. Still the sound went on and on and on…

At last Moses stood in front of them. He turned to the mountain and said something that Bezalel couldn't understand. A few seconds later, the mountain answered with another terrifying rumble. Without another word, Moses walked toward the mountain, seemingly undisturbed by its quaking, the tumbling rocks, or the thunder emanating from the cloud that obscured its top.

The people watched and waited. An hour went by, and then two. Bezalel kept looking at the place where Moses had disappeared from sight, thinking surely he would reappear any minute.

As the hours passed and Moses didn't return, people clustered around Aaron and his sons. There appeared to be a heated discussion going on.

"I'm going to see if Aaron could use my help," said Hur. Bezalel followed him through the crowd.

When they got near Aaron, Bezalel heard what sounded like an argument. "He's been gone for hours," said one of the men Bezalel recognized from the meeting of Israel's leaders. "He may have hurt himself or been injured by falling rock. We should go after him."

"I understand your concern," said Aaron, "but Moses gave me strict orders. He said under no circumstances should we go past the limits set up by these poles and rocks."

"I support Aaron," said Hur. "Today Yahweh has shown Himself powerful and frightening. We dare not risk disobeying Him by going up the mountain—even to rescue our leader."

"That's just Moses' way of keeping us servile to him," said another man in a tone of exasperation. Bezalel recognized Dathan. "If he needs our help, he'll appreciate our efforts."

"Please," said Aaron, a tone of pleading in his voice. "Please don't do this."

Bezalel had been so intent on watching the interchange that when Moses walked up behind the men, he startled. As on the day before, his face shone with such glory that Bezalel could only look at it for a minute before he had to turn away.

"Men of Israel," said Moses.

The men surrounding Aaron stepped back, shock and fear in their eyes, as if they had seen a ghost.

"I had just reached to the top of the mountain when Yahweh told me to turn around and come down. He has a message for you," said Moses.

Bezalel was sure he looked directly at Dathan as he said this.

"This is what Yahweh says," Moses continued. "'Put limits around the mountain and set it apart as holy. Do not force your way through to come to the Lord, or He will break out against you.' I told Yahweh you knew that, but He insisted I come down and tell you anyway. You weren't thinking of coming up the mountain, were you?"

Moses' sharp eyes went from one to another of the leaders and priests who surrounded Aaron. Each in turn looked down, avoiding his gaze.

"Yahweh has also told me to take Aaron to the mountaintop, but no one else is to go—not even the priests or the leaders. Listen and obey, or Yahweh will break out against you."

"We will wait for you to return," said Hur. "Today we have seen how fearful He is. We will wait for you to return with His words. Only do not have Yahweh speak to us, or we will die."

Moses and Aaron left shortly and the others went back into the crowd. Without any clear direction as to what to do next, some people left for home while others lingered on the hillside in front of the mountain.

Bezalel and Hur found a spot and sat below Sinai. Somehow, despite the fact that this place was mysterious and frightening, it was also the only place Bezalel wanted to be.

CHAPTER

twenty-eight

THE TIME OF INTENSE INTERACTION BETWEEN GOD, MOSES, AND the people continued. When Moses returned from his time on the mountain with Aaron, he called another assembly to tell the people Yahweh's further instructions.

Bezalel arrived at the meeting place with the rest of his family the morning of the assembly to see that Moses had built an altar and set up twelve pillars. "Each of these represents one of the tribes," Moses told the people through Aaron. "Choose young men from each tribe to make a sacrifice. Yahweh wants to establish His covenant with us."

It took a while for the leaders to confer and pick each tribe's representative. Then the teams of chosen men brought a young bull from their tribe to Moses and slaughtered it beside the altar. They worked together, with one inflicting the wound while the other caught in a bowl the blood that gushed from the animal's lethal wound. When the bowl was full, Moses sprinkled the remaining blood on the altar. After all the animals had been killed, their carcasses were hoisted one by one onto the altar and burned.

Bezalel watched the solemn proceedings with wonder. What did it all mean? As the smell of burning flesh and smoke drifted over the crowd, he couldn't help but think back to the Passover night when they had collected the blood in a similar way and painted it around the entrance to their homes. It had protected them from death. Was this something similar?

Finally, after the killing and burning was done, Moses and Aaron stood before the people and spoke. "These are the words Yahweh spoke to me on the mountain," Moses said. "These are the words of the covenant He makes with you: 'I am the Lord your God who brought you out of Egypt, out of the land of slavery. You shall have no other gods before Me. Do not make any gods to be alongside Me; do not make for yourselves gods of silver or gods of gold. You shall not make for yourself an idol in the form of anything in heaven above or on earth beneath or in the waters below. I am the Lord your God—a jealous God.'"

Bezalel thought of all the idols he had worked on in Egypt. He hadn't realized until now what an offense they had been to God. Maybe his broken hand was a punishment for that.

Moses continued. "You shall not misuse the name of the Lord your God. Remember the Sabbath day to keep it holy. Honor your father and your mother, so that you may live long in the land the Lord your God is giving you."

The people sat before Moses rapt, in almost complete silence.

"You shall not murder. You shall not commit adultery. You shall not steal. You shall not give false testimony against your neighbor. You shall not covet."

As Bezalel listened, a slow comprehension dawned. All that thunder, lightning, fire, and smoke on the mountain had been but a preparation for what really mattered to God. Now they knew. It was this list of simple yet challenging commands.

"This is the covenant Yahweh wants to make with you," Moses finished. "What do you say?" His burning eyes swept the crowd as he waited for their answer.

It came in a spontaneous declaration, one to which Bezalel added his voice without hesitation: "We will do everything the Lord has said. We will obey."

Now Moses directed the young men who had helped with the sacrifices to come to him. He gave them the bowls of blood collected earlier.

"Sprinkle it on the people," Moses said. "This is the blood of the covenant that the Lord has made with you in accordance with all these words."

Bezalel watched as the men circulated among the people. Now one was approaching him, beside him, passing by. A drop of blood landed on his robe. He watched as the liquid expanded and spread through the fibers of the fabric. He felt a strong sense of God's presence all around him. This was personal, a covenant between him and his God.

At the same time, he felt a tingle in his injured hand. Slowly the tingling changed to a deep, penetrating warmth. What was happening? He flexed his fingers and moved his hand from side to side. The pain was gone.

He nudged his father beside him. "My hand," he said.

"What about your hand?" asked Uri

"I'm having the strangest sensations in it," said Bezalel, "and the pain's not there anymore. Will you help me take off my bandage?"

They unwrapped the linen strips that held the splints in place and removed them. Underneath was a hand that was unbruised and straight. No one would ever have guessed that it had been broken. Yahweh had healed his hand!

* * *

The next day, messengers came for Hur. God had given Moses instructions to take Israel's leaders up on the mountain. Bezalel looked with longing after Hur as he left their tent. After what had happened the day before, he wished he could go with them. The next best thing would be to visit Oholiab.

"No bandage?" asked Oholiab as he welcomed Bezalel into the tent.

"No bandage—and look!" Bezalel held up his right hand, turned and twisted it, wriggled and flexed his fingers.

"It's better!" exclaimed Oholiab, looking shocked. "What happened?"

Bezalel told him the story of how his hand had been healed in an instant during the previous day's covenant ceremony. "The whole day felt like a holy encounter," he said. "When Moses was naming Yahweh's requirements, I felt especially guilty when he spoke of making idols. That was my life in Egypt, the main thing for which I used my hands. I had no idea that what I did was such an offense to Him. When He restored my broken hand yesterday, I sensed that He forgave me and was giving me a new start. I feel a great thankfulness and I've made a new resolve. From now on, I want to serve and honor only Yahweh with my hands."

"That is a new start," said Oholiab. "You don't know how encouraging your story is to me, for I too felt convicted when Moses declared God's rules. When I see something beautiful, I want it. The words 'You shall not covet' went straight to my heart. Your sense of being forgiven gives me hope that Yahweh may forgive me too, and use me in spite of my faults."

"Remember how last time I was here you talked of my broken hand as a test?" asked Bezalel. "I feel like my test ended yesterday. Perhaps recognizing your covetousness was also a test. Do you suppose we have now passed Yahweh's tests? Could it be that His time to show us how we can use our skills for Him will come soon?"

"I hope so," said Oholiab. "Oh, how I hope so."

* * *

It was late that evening when Hur returned. He looked dazed and greeted the family in a distracted way. Noemi gave him the manna she had prepared for the evening meal and he sat on the tent floor, eating.

The whole family, anticipating his return, had gathered around to hear his report. But now they watched him in respectful silence.

Finally, Uri spoke. "Your time on the mountain with Moses, how was it?"

For a minute, Hur looked at him as if in a trance. Then he began to cry, trickling tears that grew to sobs, then shuddering gasps.

Everyone looked on in shocked surprise. Bezalel had never before seen his grandfather cry. Noemi went to him and rubbed his back as if comforting a child.

Gradually Hur's sobbing calmed. "I'm sorry," he said at last, "but this day has stirred me to the deepest parts. We saw Yahweh. He is beyond description—brighter than the sun, radiant and glorious. Before Him I felt utterly small and dirty. And I saw my faults. Especially my pride. I was proud to be there, chosen to judge Israel, and in that instant I understood how much Yahweh hates such a spirit. But at the same time, I felt His love. He saw me with all my rottenness, but still let me linger in His presence."

"Was He scary, like the mountain?" asked Zamri.

"No," said Hur. "He was—oh, how could I describe Him? Other. Beyond what I thought or imagined. It's hard to compare Him to anything we know. That time on the mountain with Him was like nothing I've ever experienced. In some ways, it's like the climax of my life—as if all my days so far have been a journey leading toward that meeting."

His grandfather's description reminded Bezalel of the feelings he'd had during yesterday's ceremony. What did these wonderful things mean?

"We ate together," Hur went on.

"What did you eat?" asked Noemi.

"It was the finest meat, bread, and fruit with dates, nuts, and honeycomb. And wine."

Bezalel couldn't help but think of Oholiab. Wouldn't he have relished such a spread!

"The meeting was over too soon," said Hur. He sighed. "Moses sent us down the mountain while he and Joshua stayed. He has asked me to help Aaron settle any disputes that rise among the people."

"You mean you're one of the top judges now?" asked Zamri.

"I don't think of it that way," said Hur. "After today, top or bottom is nothing. Pleasing Yahweh is the only thing that matters. And my assignment is only until Moses gets back. It will probably be for just a few days."

The talk of judging brought Bezalel back to his present situation with a thud. In the last few days, he had all but forgotten about Ethan's threat to bring him before the elders. But that matter still wasn't settled. Was Hur's pride about to receive another blow because of him?

CHAPTER

twenty-nine

As he walked with Grandpa Hur to the place of meeting, Bezalel was plagued by fear. Would Dathan and Ethan be there to make their complaint? If so, whose side of the story would Aaron believe? Grandpa Hur had told Bezalel that he would remove himself from passing judgment on someone from his own family. What would his punishment be if Aaron didn't believe him? Bezalel was fearful of what awaited him, but also determined to face whatever was ahead and get it over with.

Moses had been gone for several days now and Hur was going to help Aaron with the judging duties. However, when they arrived at the place of meeting, no one was waiting. They went on to Aaron's tent. There, a servant told them he was busy and there would be no judging session today. Bezalel felt relieved, but also disappointed. He wanted the matter settled.

In the following days, the delay continued. Though Hur continued going to the place of meeting each morning, Aaron had yet to convene the type of tribunal Moses had officiated at daily. He seemed occupied with other matters.

After Moses had been gone for a week, Hur, Uri, and Bezalel saw that instead of people assembling in the public meeting area, there was a long line outside Aaron's tent. It seemed he was meeting people inside and holding private conversations.

"What do you think is going on?" asked Bezalel.

"I don't know," said Hur. "But something about it makes me uneasy."

One week turned into two. Still Moses didn't return. Bezalel went with Uri and Hur several more times to see if Aaron was ready to convene the judging. Each time they encountered a similar scene outside Aaron's tent.

Other things were changing in the camp as well. People were forgetting to pick extra manna on the day before Sabbath, then borrowing from neighbors the food they had neglected to gather for themselves. Bezalel sensed a general air of discontent. As he passed tents, he overheard arguments. When he was gathering manna, all around him were the sounds of muttering and grumbling. When he went for water, the curses he heard leveled at Moses and the other leaders made him lower his head for fear that he would be recognized as Hur's grandson.

He struggled with a restlessness of his own. The days felt long without work to fill them. He had promised to use his talents for Yahweh, but what did that mean practically? Should he no longer make jewelry? He felt like going back to the shop and resuming his former work, yet he also felt an internal check about that. Wouldn't that be setting himself up for the temptation of again working to earn the praise of people?

And there was the whole issue of covetousness. He had thought a lot about covetousness since Oholiab had identified it as a flaw in himself. When he made beautiful finery, wasn't he encouraging covetousness in others? If these things displeased Yahweh, wasn't he going back on his promise if he continued making them?

One day, he went to see Shoshan.

"Your hand is completely recovered?" His friend seemed surprised. "That was fast!"

"It happened in an instant," said Bezalel, telling Shoshan about the miracle healing.

"Are you back at work?"

"No. I haven't touched my tools since I put them away after Ethan injured me. But I've thought about it. Have the craftsmen set up a common workplace again?"

"They have," said Shoshan, "though I haven't joined them. Shall we pay them a visit?"

"Yes, let's."

* * *

The workplace at the edge of camp resembled the ones they had set up at Elim and Rephidim, only this one was bigger. As they approached, Bezalel saw that some of the men had set out their creations on mats, market-style. Examining their work, Bezalel saw that along with representations of flowers and fruits, there were many pendants, rings, and bracelets inscribed with ankhs, eyes of Horus, scarabs, and other Egyptian symbols.

Some women were trying on armbands and collars. As Bezalel watched, an argument broke out between two of them.

"I had that bracelet first," said one, reaching out to take the gold circlet another woman had in her hand.

"You put it down, so I have as much right to it as you do," said the other, holding it above her head, out of reach.

"Give it to me. It looks way better on me…"

Bezalel left as they began tussling over the trinket.

In the work area were many workmen he had never met before, but also some he recognized. He greeted his old friends, but there was a coolness in their response that surprised him. He spotted Abnosh and went over to him, but the man obviously wasn't happy to see him.

"Have you come back to lord it over us?" he asked.

"Lord it over you?" answered Bezalel. "I never lorded it over you."

"We wouldn't listen to you, in any case," said Abnosh. "Sneak. Liar. Ethan will have his revenge on you yet!"

Bezalel was glad to get away. If there had been any question about whether it was a good idea to go back to work here, the matter was now settled. He could never do that again—at least, not in this setting.

* * *

When Moses had been away for an entire month, Hur, Uri, and Bezalel walked to the meeting place again to find Aaron talking with a group of Israel's leaders. This time, they were meeting under a canopy pitched beside his tent.

Bezalel knew Hur had not been told of this meeting. The three of them sat at the outskirts of the group and listened as one after another spoke.

"He's probably had an accident," said one. "He's not a young man and that mountain is a treacherous place."

"I suggest that God has destroyed him," said another. "You know how fearful Yahweh appeared that day on the mountain, and how Moses himself warned us against going up on it. God has probably visited the same fate on Moses."

"I think we need to look ahead." The speaker was Dathan. "Obviously Moses isn't coming back. We need a new leader."

"And since Moses was our link to Yahweh, we have lost our connection to the Almighty," said another man. "With another leader, we need another god."

As the men kept talking, Bezalel sensed that his grandfather was becoming more and more agitated.

Finally, Hur stood up and called out, "Men of Israel, what are you doing? Don't you remember our promise to keep God's laws as Moses spoke them to us? How dare you say such things?"

Aaron and the others looked around, then exchanged glances with each other, as if asking how *he* happened to be there.

"Don't worry, Hur," said Aaron. "The men just wanted a meeting to air their concerns. I'm sure we'll come to some sort of agreement that's satisfactory to everyone. In fact, maybe you have a solution for us to consider."

Bezalel shuddered at the condescending tone in his voice, the smile on his face, and the crafty glance he exchanged with Dathan.

Hur, if he had noticed these things, didn't let on. Instead, he took the invitation at face value. "For one, I don't think we should give up on Moses. Think how often on this journey things have taken longer than expected. Yahweh is teaching us to be patient. Maybe with this delay He is testing us to see if our trust is truly in Him. It is He, not Moses, who is really behind our release from bondage. Your talk of replacing Yahweh with other gods is frightening. Have you forgotten your promise to Moses and God not thirty days ago? And how could any other god do better for us? Have you heard of any other god who has defeated the Egyptians? Or opened up a sea for people to walk across? Or supplied bread in the desert, or water from a rock?"

There was silence among the men. They looked uncomfortable and shifted nervously.

Finally, Aaron broke the awkward silence. "Thank you, Hur. We will keep your comments in mind. Now, does anyone else have something to say?"

"Let's go," muttered Hur, still standing from having given his speech. Uri and Bezalel stood and the three turned to leave. Bezalel felt the eyes of the assembled men drilling into his back as they walked toward their tent.

PART FIVE

Chosen

CHAPTER *thirty*

"WHY ARE YOU MOPING?" ASKED NOEMI. "WHY AREN'T YOU WORKING on the things that used to keep you busy?"

"I can't," said Bezalel.

"Why not? Your hand is well. Everyone likes your work."

Moses had been gone for over a month, the atmosphere in the camp had continued to deteriorate, and Bezalel was feeling increasingly restless and irritable. Despite the lawless conditions, he had no liberty. Every time he felt the urge to take out his tools, an internal check stopped him.

"It's not because people don't like what I do," he said, "but because of a promise I made to Yahweh. When He healed my hand, I vowed to use it to serve Him alone."

"What are you talking about?" asked Noemi, staring at him incredulously. "You mean you're going to waste the rest of your life because of a promise you made in an emotional moment?"

"The things I make only stir up pride in me," said Bezalel, trying to get her to understand. "I can't make those trinkets anymore."

"Be practical," said Noemi. "Think of it another way. It might not be a bad thing to use your skill to gain a little good will among the people for the day Dathan and Ethan bring their accusation against you to the judges. As for your promise to Yahweh, Moses has been gone for a very long time and the people are saying Yahweh may have killed him and forsaken us."

It disturbed Bezalel to hear his mother say these things. To ease his restlessness, he went out for a walk. He wandered to the plain where God had met them only weeks before and tried to relive the sensation of Yahweh's presence. Here, at the foot of the mountain, it had seemed real enough to touch. But today he felt nothing.

He looked up at the top of the mountain, still covered in cloud. Had Yahweh really forsaken them? Was Moses gone for good?

* * *

Bezalel's restless thoughts spilled into his dreams. That night, he dreamt that he was back in Khafra's shop. Khafra stood beside him as he put the finishing touches on a calf idol. He looked in admiration at the work. "You were destined to do this," he said.

In his dream, Bezalel left the shop and found himself walking back to the slave encampment. But he couldn't see. It was the night of the plague of darkness and he kept tripping and bumping into things. The trumpet sound of the day Yahweh came down on the mountain sounded and his sense of urgency increased. He was supposed to be at the foot of the mountain with the people, but he couldn't find his way.

His heart pounding in panic, he awoke.

When he fell back to sleep, he dreamed Khafra was there again. But then he became Moses, who looked right through Bezalel with his terrible eyes. "Yahweh has a destiny for your hands," Moses said. "He has seen your heart. Very soon you will get your desire."

In his dream, Bezalel saw mounds of gold, all kinds of jewelry, trinkets, and items of silver and bronze, colorful weavings, dyed animal skins, carvings, and precious stones. Light streamed from the cloud and shone on the treasure heap. He awoke with the same sense of well-being he'd had when he first sat in Yahweh's presence at the foot of the mountain. The feeling of the dream lasted into the next morning. He held it close, not telling anyone.

* * *

Grandpa Hur seemed restless too. He wanted to see what was happening where the people met at Aaron's tent, so Bezalel and Uri accompanied him there. As they made their way through the camp, they met others who were also on their way to Aaron's tent.

When they got there, they were met with the strangest sight. People were bringing pieces of gold and silver—amulets, rings, collars, bracelets, armbands—and tossing them on a pile while several of Israel's leaders watched and stood guard. The collection had obviously gone on for a while, for the mound was high, reaching to Bezalel's knees. As he looked at it, he felt a jolt of recognition. It resembled the scene in his dream.

"What is this about?" Hur asked a man who had just finished dropping a collection of gold armbands on the pile.

"Aaron has commanded it," said the man.

"Where is he? I want to speak with him," said Hur.

Hur approached Aaron's tent, past the men guarding the pile. Though Bezalel and Uri hung back, Bezalel saw one of the men block his way.

"Aaron isn't here," the man said.

"Where is he?" Hur asked.

"We don't know."

"I must see him," Hur exclaimed. He took a few steps toward the tent as if to enter it anyway, but again the man who had halted him came between him and the opening.

"You cannot see him," the man said. "He told us not to let anyone in. He is resting."

Hur turned away and walked back toward their tent. Uri and Bezalel followed. Bezalel had never seen him look so distraught.

"Aaron, Aaron, what are you doing?" Hur muttered under his breath. "What is this thing you are planning to do?"

Late that evening, a messenger came to their tent. Bezalel was already lying on his sleeping mat when he arrived. He heard voices and assumed the message would be for Hur. But then Uri came to where Bezalel was lying. "Aaron has sent for you," he said.

"For me? What could he want with me?"

"I don't know," said Uri. "You'd better go and find out."

Bezalel jumped up, dressed, and joined the messenger outside in the cold desert night. "Do you know what Aaron wants?" he asked the man who had come for him. "Is something wrong?"

"I'm not sure," said the messenger. "All I know is that Aaron very much wants to see you."

When they got to Aaron's tent, Bezalel saw that the pile of gold and trinkets had grown to twice the height it had been earlier in the day. He thought of Hur's reaction to Aaron's plan and felt a shiver go through him. What could this have to do with him?

"Welcome to my tent, Bezalel, grandson of my friend Hur. I'm sorry about the lateness of the hour," Aaron greeted him. He had never shown Bezalel such familiarity and warmth before.

"I wasn't yet asleep," said Bezalel. "What is it you want?"

"I have heard many things about you," Aaron began. "Word is that you are a skilled craftsman. People praise your work." His tone was cloying in its sweetness. As he spoke, his eyes never left Bezalel's face but searched it as if to gauge the effect his words were having.

When Bezalel gave no response, Aaron continued. "I have a proposition for you. As you know, Moses has disappeared. We're sure he is dead and gone for good, perhaps from an animal attack or an accident on the mountain. Perhaps he was even killed at the hand of Yahweh. Now the people are clamoring for a new god. I'm afraid of what they'll do if I don't give them what they want, so I have collected gold and trinkets from them. With your skill and experience in Egypt, I believe you would be the perfect one to cast this image. Would you do this for me?"

As Aaron's request became clear, Bezalel felt a cold chill go through him. His grandfather would be incensed. He himself couldn't imagine saying yes, and yet the person asking him to do this was Aaron, Moses' brother, a leader and a man he had always respected! The image of the pile of gold from his dream and the prediction that he would use his talents to fulfill his heart's desire flashed into his mind. This couldn't be the fulfillment of that, could it?

"Uh… uh…" He tried desperately to think of a way he could phrase his refusal in polite terms. "Sir, I don't think I could do this. Hasn't Yahweh forbidden us to make images of worship?"

"I understand your hesitation," said Aaron. "But you must know that with the disappearance of Moses, the people are begging for change. How can they be expected to follow Yahweh and His rules if His servant Moses is no longer alive? So they're asking for a god with power to take His place. I'm sure you will remember the power of the Egyptian gods. In fact, in your service of Pharaoh, didn't you help form them?"

"Yes, I did," said Bezalel. "But that was before Moses came and showed us the power of Yahweh. I could never defy His rules like that."

"Oh, but that wouldn't really be defying Him. You don't have to bow down to the image yourself," said Aaron. "Making it would be using your talents in the service of your people. Just make the idol to keep peace and order in the camp."

"I… I couldn't," said Bezalel. He looked down, not wanting to look Aaron in the face.

"Hmmm. Suppose I sweeten the offer?" Aaron's tone changed and Bezalel looked up to see cunning in his eyes. "I hear that you've set your heart on a certain young woman whom another young man also wants to marry. In fact, I have heard that a complaint of indecent behavior toward her is pending against you. If you make this idol for me, I'll see to it that all the complaints are quashed. The case will never be heard and you will be free to marry the girl if that's what you and your parents wish."

The offer took the breath out of Bezalel. For the work of a few days, he could get rid of the worry of Ethan's case against him and gain Sebia as his betrothed? It was too good to be true.

Maybe he should accept. If Moses was indeed gone, what would it matter? And he would again have the purpose of a task to perform, not to mention a reason to take out his tools and work with his beloved gold. He could again use the skills honed in Egypt on just such projects. He would never need to tell anyone, just cast and form it secretly and, when the job was done, pretend he knew nothing of it.

Aaron took Bezalel's silence for agreement. "Good! We must get right to work! I've already collected the wood to fire bricks for the kiln. Wait here while I get the men started on it."

Bezalel sat alone in Aaron's tent, feeling shaken. Was he doing the right thing? He thought of the black night of Egypt when he had promised Yahweh his life. Then, only weeks ago, Yahweh had healed his hand. Even if Moses never came back, he knew God was real because he had felt His healing touch. How could he now do this thing God had specifically forbidden? Besides, would Sebia even want him if she found out what he had done to win her?

Aaron returned shortly, looking pleased. "Now, tell me what else you need, so I can get you outfitted for the job—"

"I can't," Bezalel cut in. "No matter what happens with the complaint against me, even if I never get Sebia as my wife, I cannot disobey Yahweh like this."

The tone of Aaron's voice became pleading. "Oh, come now. I have everything ready. Please? For me? For the people? For your family?"

"My family?" said Bezalel. "If my grandfather knew of it, he would be furious."

"You wouldn't have to tell him. It's the only way I can keep control of the people. You won't let me down, will you?"

Bezalel felt miserable. He hated confrontation. Defying a person in authority went against everything inside him. But there was no other way.

"I can't do it," he said.

The smile on Aaron's face froze and his tone turned cold. "You're sure? You won't change your mind?"

Bezalel shook his head, not daring to look up into Aaron's face.

"Then get out!" The command was quiet but sharp. "I was ready to do a great deal for you. But your stubbornness and ingratitude make that impossible. Get out now—and you'll be sorry!"

Bezalel left the tent and scurried home. The acrid smell of smoke burned his nose and throat. The desert night had never felt darker.

"TOMORROW WILL BE A FESTIVAL TO THE LORD!" THREE DAYS LATER, messengers ran through the camp shouting the announcement.

Aaron actually went through with it, Bezalel thought with a sinking heart.

The day after Aaron had called Bezalel to his tent, he told his family about Aaron's request. In the intervening days, Bezalel had listened with dismay as news of a golden calf statue spread throughout the camp. And now Aaron was calling it a festival to the Lord.

The discussion at their evening meal that night was whether or not to attend the festivity.

"I don't want to be seen to support this in any way," said Hur. "But on the other hand, I feel responsible for the people. Moses asked me to help Aaron in this. Though he didn't accept any of my advice, I feel like I need to know what's going on."

"Let's hope this doesn't become like the celebrations in Egypt," said Uri. "If it does, things will get rowdy. Noemi, Zamri, and I will stay away."

"But all my friends are going," wailed Zamri.

"I don't think *all* your friends," said Noemi. "I was speaking with Cetura's mother. They're confused about this. I'm sure Cetura will be staying away with the rest of her family."

Bezalel felt torn. On the one hand, he wanted to have nothing to do with this idolatrous festival. On the other, he sided with Hur, feeling in some way responsible. Maybe if he had been more persuasive, he could have dissuaded Aaron from doing this. He would go with Hur to watch the next day's festivities.

The two of them got up early and joined the crowds that thronged to the meeting place at the edge of the camp. Many were dressed in fancy Egyptian clothes and wore the extravagant Egyptian headbands, earrings, collars, and necklaces they had taken from their neighbors just months before. Some led sheep and cattle, and now animal calls mingled with the laughter and excited chatter filling the air.

When they arrived, Bezalel saw the golden calf idol. It was crudely made by craftsman standards but still had a bovine resemblance. It was elevated on a platform in the middle of the open square. In front of it was a stone altar. Aaron stood beside the altar, greeting the people and designating assistants to take charge of the animals brought to him. The people crowded around the calf and the altar, forming a large circle in front of it.

Just beyond the flat plain, where the people had gathered, was hilly terrain with large boulders. Bezalel and Hur clambered to a vantage place on the rocks in order to see all that went on.

When the crowd was thick, Aaron began the festivities, shouting into a trumpet that amplified his words, "Welcome, O Israel. Welcome to the first festival of your new god." He pointed toward the calf idol. "O Israel, this is your god who brought you out of Egypt. Let us sacrifice and offer burnt and fellowship offerings to it."

Trumpets sounded and the men who had taken the animals paraded them to the altar. There, others slaughtered them and hoisted their bodies onto the fire that was burning on the altar. All the while, the people looked on and cheered. Some began dancing around the altar, as the Egyptians had done during their festivals, and shouted out prayers and incantations of the kind Bezalel had heard in Egypt.

As he watched, Bezalel thought of the sacrifice at Sinai just over a month ago when Moses had spoken God's laws. What had become of the promise the whole nation had made to remain loyal to God? He looked down and saw where his tunic was still stained with the spatters of blood that had sealed his promise to Yahweh. Dark disappointment overwhelmed him. If Moses was gone, what was God's plan for them now?

When all the animals had been sacrificed, some men took partially burned carcasses off the altar and began to carve them. Soon there was a crowd around them, begging for meat. Another crowd formed around a man who had jugs and was filling people's water skins and bowls with drink. People brought out instruments—lyres, timbrels, cymbals, and drums. Presently the music of Egypt filled the air and people danced around in front of the altar and the golden idol.

"I can't stand to look," said Hur. Tears glistened in his eyes.

Bezalel's attention was drawn from the crowd to scanning it for individuals. So far he hadn't seen any of his friends—like Oholiab, Shoshan, or Benjamin—among the revelers. But now he spotted some who looked familiar—Abnosh and Ethan. Ethan was with a girl. Could it be? Yes, it was! Sebia. He was leading her in a line dance, though she seemed to be resisting. They stopped, talked to each other in a spirited way, and then Sebia broke away from him and ran into the crowd.

Bezalel squinted, trying to catch sight of her again. He caught a glimpse as she ran through a place where the crowd was thin, but then the people milling around obscured her. She appeared to be heading toward the edge of the camp and the canopies that people had set up as shelters from the hot sun.

"I just saw someone I know," he said to Hur. "I must go down."

He leapt from rock to rock as he descended from their lookout. He dashed from one shelter to the next, looking for Sebia. He was about to give up when he heard sobbing. Looking around, he saw a tangle of blankets. As he studied it, he saw it move ever so slightly; the sound seemed to be coming from it. He lifted the blanket to reveal Sebia, lying curled on the ground, her shoulders shaking with sobs.

Bezalel touched her shoulder. "Sebia," he said softly.

She stopped crying, sat up, and rubbed the tears from her eyes. "Bezalel, what are you doing here?"

"I was watching the celebration with my grandfather from the hillside," he replied. "I saw you with Ethan. And then I saw you run from him."

She took a deep, ragged breath. "Ethan made me come. His father was one of the people who convinced Aaron to do this. It's all so horrible!"

"I know," said Bezalel. "It's the last thing I thought would happen. After all we've seen Yahweh do, to return to the gods of Egypt? It's unthinkable."

"And how have you been?" Sebia asked, looking at him. Her lovely eyes were swollen and she looked like the embodiment of misery.

"Alright," he said. "Although I've stopped making things out of gold. It just gets me into trouble."

"I'm so sorry," she said. "Ethan found what you gave me. I still don't know how. He was terribly angry. He convinced my father to join with him and his father to bring a charge against you, even though I told them you hadn't even touched me. Ethan wouldn't believe it. I haven't given my assent to the betrothal, but they're going ahead with wedding plans as though I have."

"Oh," said Bezalel. He felt a deep dismay. "When will they bring the charge against me?"

"I don't know," said Sebia. "My father has been stalling. He probably doesn't want to draw too much attention to me." She looked down now, as if unable to look him in the eye. "You see, I have a past of my own."

"I remember you referred to it once," said Bezalel, "but you never told me what it was. Please tell me."

"When we were in Egypt, my master abused me," Sebia said. She kept looking down. "I'm not the virgin you thought I was. My parents are afraid that if I come under too much scrutiny, the truth will come out and no one will want to marry me."

Bezalel stared at her in silence. *No! How can this be true? So my mother was right. Sebia does have a past… she isn't the innocent woman she appears to be. How can I have been fooled all this time?*

"It was Yahweh who rescued me from that pit," she went on. "I prayed and prayed and He answered my prayer by sending Moses. That's why I danced the way I did after crossing the Red Sea. It was a thank-you to Yahweh for freeing me of my Egyptian master. And now we're back to this. I feel the darkness of Egypt closing in again. It's all so confusing." She buried her face in her hands and her shoulders shook with silent sobs. "Ethan will be so angry when he finds out what I am. And what must you think? I'm sorry I kept this from you. I've wanted to tell you since the day you gave me the gift."

As he looked down at her, he felt disenchantment—and pity. He could only imagine what Ethan would do when he found out about her. Or maybe Ethan would just reject her and she'd be free to marry him. But now did he even want to?

BEZALEL WAS SUDDENLY AWARE OF SILENCE. THE MUSIC HAD STOPPED and it was strangely still.

"What's going on?" he asked. He stood and stretched as tall as he could. "I have to go. Something has happened to quiet the party."

She got to her feet as if to join him, but he motioned for her to stay.

"Don't come with me," he said. "It will just get you into trouble. But I pray Yahweh will put everything right for you—and me."

He thought of pushing through the crowds around the altar, but decided against it. Instead he climbed back up to the hillside viewpoint.

Hur was nowhere around, but a few others were present. From up here, he had a good view of the action on the plain below.

He saw a man, his arms laden with pieces of shattered stone tablet, lumbering across the plain. Was that Joshua?

There appeared to be some kind of a standoff in front of the calf and the altar. He strained to recognize who was involved. It looked like Moses! Had Moses returned? Even as he stared, he saw Moses move toward the golden calf and push it onto the ground.

Bezalel scrambled down the rocks, eager to see what was going on at close range. Even before he got near, he heard Moses' booming voice: "What did these people do to you that you led them into such great sin?"

A red-faced Aaron was obviously the target of Moses' questions.

"Do not be angry, my lord," Aaron said. "You know how prone these people are to evil. They said to me, 'Make us gods who will go before us. As for this fellow Moses, who brought us up out of Egypt, we don't know what has happened to him.' So I told them, 'Whoever has any gold jewelry, take it off.' Then they gave me the gold, I threw it into the fire, and out came this calf."

Despite Moses' presence, a cheer went up from the crowd after Aaron said this. Moses turned and walked away from the unruly, drunken partiers who had again taken up their instruments to cavort and sing before the now-fallen idol.

Moses walked to the edge of the camp and shouted, "Whoever is for the Lord, come to me."

Bezalel hurried over and stood with the group forming around Moses. In a few minutes, a crowd had gathered. Many were Levites of Moses' own tribe. To them, Moses said, "This is what the Lord, the God of Israel, says: 'Each man strap a sword to his side. Go back and forth through the camp from one end to the other, each killing his brother and friend and neighbor.'"

* * *

The rest of that day, and the days immediately following, were a blur to Bezalel. The aftermath in the camp was almost unthinkable as those loyal to Moses went against their brothers and sisters. At the end of the slaughter, over three thousand had been killed.

Moses' terrible anger hadn't ended there. He had burned the calf in a hot fire, then ground the gold into dust and sprinkled it into the drinking water so that everyone in the camp was reminded of the close brush with idolatry they had just avoided.

Through all these events, Bezalel thought often of Sebia. He tried to sort out his feelings for her now that he knew the truth. She had once belonged to someone else. But she had been forced into that relationship, hadn't she? He recalled her words: "I danced a thank-you to Yahweh for freeing me of my Egyptian master." Still, it was hard to believe she wasn't who he had imagined her to be all along. Could he love her anyway?

* * *

"You have committed a great sin, but now I will go up to the Lord. Perhaps I can make atonement." Moses looked old, weary, and troubled as he addressed the crowd at a meeting a few days later.

What a different congregation gathered now. The backtalk and sarcasm were absent. People who had come from burying their newly dead wept openly. Gaiety and singing had turned to sadness and weeping.

Aaron was absent from Moses' side. Bezalel wondered what his fate would be. Joshua was nearby, but Moses spoke for himself. Moses then left the camp, but the heaviness of his concern lingered over the people.

Even though he had resisted Aaron's request and not bowed to the golden image, Bezalel felt the weight of it. It had taken Moses' return to drive home how serious their transgression against Yahweh was.

Hours later, Moses came back. The people who had waited at the meeting place grew still as he came before them. "This is what God says: 'Whoever has sinned against Me, I will blot out of My book. Now go, lead the people to the place I spoke of. And My angel will go before you. When the time comes for Me to punish, I will punish them for their sin.'"

As Bezalel left the assembly with his family, he wondered how God's punishment would show itself. Not twenty-four hours later, scores of people in the camp were sick with plague.

* * *

"Shalom."

Bezalel looked up from gathering manna to see Sebia beside him. Despite his confused thoughts over the last few days, his heart jumped at the sight of her.

"Shalom," he answered. "It's good to see you."

Her eyes looked tired and her face pale, as if she had been ill. A longing to protect her arose in him.

"You look troubled," he said.

"My family has been sick with plague," she replied. "But even more has happened. Ethan was killed in the massacre."

Bezalel was stunned by the news. He studied Sebia. How did she feel about this? Even as he gazed at her, her eyes filled her eyes.

"I don't know why I'm sad," she said, starting to cry. "I never wanted to be betrothed to him. But he's gone now and it has all been so very frightening."

"I know what you mean," said Bezalel. "It's only now that I realize how serious Yahweh is about us being true to Him."

"I should have tried harder to persuade him against worshiping that idol," said Sebia. "If only I had known it would be so fatal."

"Yahweh will deal justly with him in the afterlife, as He will deal kindly with you," Bezalel said, looking long and deep into her tear-filled eyes.

thirty-three

At last it seemed that Moses had completely won the hearts of the people. He set up a tent at the edge of the camp and met with Yahweh there. He called it the tent of meeting and invited people to bring their requests to him so he could bring them to the Lord.

Whenever he went to speak with Yahweh in this manner, the cloud descended from the top of the mountain and hovered at the entrance of his tent. Now, instead of making sarcastic remarks about him going off and meeting with God as they had before, people stood at the entrances of their tents, looking with awe at the cloud of Yahweh's presence, and worshiped.

One day after spending time with God in this way, Moses called another assembly.

"Yahweh has told me to come up to Him on the mountain again," he said. "Perhaps He will again write His laws on tablets to replace the ones I broke when I witnessed your idolatry. No one is to come with me. Aaron and your leaders will take charge. Do not run wild again."

Bezalel felt dread at Moses' announcement. What would happen this time? Would the people convince Aaron to compromise again?

Now almost every morning he and Sebia met while gathering manna. He talked to her about his fears.

"I don't think it's the same," she reassured him. "I may be wrong, but one person who resisted Moses' leadership has been silent. Dathan and his friends Abiram and Korah, who were once vocal opponents, have been very quiet lately."

"I guess we just have to trust Moses' wisdom and hope that Aaron has learned from last time," said Bezalel.

"Well, we both know he won't get any help from you!"

Bezalel smiled at that. Now that he felt free to get to know her, he was coming to see what a treasure Sebia really was. And he knew that he wanted more than these casual meetings.

* * *

That morning, after the family had eaten their first manna of the day, Bezalel hauled out the robe that held his tools. Even looking at that old garment brought back a flood of memories. As he unwrapped the cloth to reveal the tongs, crucible, bellows, wax, smoothing stone, and all his carving tools, a flood of warmth came over him. These tools were a part of who he was. How he had missed them!

A linen parcel lay among the tools. He took it up, untied it, and looked again at the gift he had given Sebia. It was as beautiful a piece of work as he had ever done, he thought as his fingers traced the honeycomb pattern. He examined the place where it had been pulled apart. It wouldn't take much to fix it. An hour or so and it would be as good as new.

Too soon, the necklace was mended and he looked around. Could he make something else while he had his tools out? It felt so good to use his hands again. But at the first thoughts of the things he could make, he sensed again that inner check. He had been here before. Always the path had led toward an unwelcome and unintended end. He had vowed he was done with all this. How could he even think of going back to it?

He rewrapped Sebia's repaired necklace in the linen. At least he had confidence in this thing he had made, for it expressed his heart's affection. He was sure that on Sebia the pieces would do nothing but good—and this time he would win her in the acceptable way.

The very next morning, he talked to his father and mother about Sebia and his desire to marry her. That put in motion the negotiations that would soon make her his betrothed.

* * *

Bezalel's eyes lit up as he saw his beautiful bride-to-be coming across the desert plain with her manna basket. They had been betrothed for several weeks now, and each day was a new adventure as he got to know Sebia a little better. She had become his best friend and confidante as they told each other about their lives in Egypt and their hopes and dreams once they got to the Promised Land.

However, even his new relationship with Sebia hadn't solved all his problems. He had not taken out his tools since the day he had repaired her necklace—though the temptation came to him often. Some days, the desire to again realize the pleasure of making something with his hands almost got the best of him. But then he remembered his promise to Yahweh. The pile of treasure he had seen in his dream, followed so closely by Aaron's request and the sight of that pile beside Aaron's tent, must have been some kind of warning. How could he now resume his gold working and not feel he was in danger of compromise?

Suddenly, Moses was back. The news of his arrival reached their tent and Hur said he wanted to welcome him. Bezalel went along.

Moses was soon surrounded by those wishing to greet him. His face shone almost too brightly, as it had at other times when he had been with Yahweh. Bezalel wondered what it would feel like to be so close to God that He would speak to him and display His visible glory.

Soon after he got back to the camp, Moses called a meeting of the elders.

Hur returned from the meeting, all smiles. "Moses has again met with Yahweh," he told the family. "He has come back with God's words carved into new tablets to replace those he smashed when he witnessed the calf idol."

The next day, Moses summoned all the people for an assembly.

As Bezalel walked through the camp to the meeting place with his family, he sensed hope and joy. Gone was the pall of guilt and the misery that had followed the camp's punishment. Today there was an air of openness and a buzz of anticipation.

The crowd settled and Moses rose to speak. He showed them the tablets of stone he had carried down from the mountain; they were covered in writing.

"These are God's words to me," he said, raising them high. "Despite your sin, God has not given up on you. This is what He said to me: 'The Lord, the Lord, the compassionate and gracious God, slow to anger, abounding in love and faithfulness, maintaining love to thousands, and forgiving wickedness, rebellion and sin.'"

Then he read the rules the people had heard only three months before. He also related new commandments.

"Celebrate the Feast of Unleavened Bread in the month of Nisan, for in that month you came out of Egypt. Celebrate the Feast of Weeks. Only do not tempt God again with idolatry, for He is also completely just. He will deal with each of you according to what you have done. He says, 'Yet I do not leave the guilty unpunished; I punish the children and their children for the sin of the parents to the third and fourth generation.'"

Bezalel listened, alert and attentive, for these were the words of Yahweh, the God to whom he had pledged his life. Suddenly he knew that what he wanted more than anything else was to experience the intimacy with God that Moses had. But it meant he had to deal once and for all with the only thing that could compete with Yahweh for his affections.

That night, he again opened the package that held his tools. He looked at them, then lifted each one to feel its familiar heft and caress the smoothness of the metal, stone, and wood. He then wrapped them tight and put them beside his mat. Next to the parcel, he placed a small shovel. He would leave at first light. By tomorrow night, his dilemma would be buried in the sand a good half-day's journey away.

thirty-four

BEZALEL WOKE THE NEXT MORNING TO DAYLIGHT AND THE CLAMOR OF voices. He had overslept. The family was up, hurrying around. Moses had called another assembly. Everyone was to gather at the meeting place at the edge of camp.

He took his tools and the shovel he had prepared the night before and shoved them under his mattress. His trip would have to wait for another day.

This morning, Moses repeated the command to keep the Sabbath as a day of rest and went on. "From what you have, take an offering for

Yahweh. Everyone who is willing is to bring to Yahweh an offering of gold, silver and bronze, yarn of blue, purple and scarlet, goat hair and ram skins dyed red, acacia wood, olive oil for the light, spices for the anointing oil and for the fragrant incense, onyx stones and other gems…"

Bezalel listened, transfixed. Moses was naming the exact things he had seen in his dream.

His speech continued. "All who are skilled among you are to come and make everything Yahweh has commanded: the tabernacle with its tent and its covering, clasps, frames, crossbars, posts, and bases; the ark with its poles and the atonement cover and the curtain that shields it; the table with its poles and all its articles and the bread of the Presence; the lamp stand that is for light with its accessories, lamps and oil for the light…"

Bezalel felt dazed. Was he hearing right? Moses was describing a worship place that needed things made of gold, bronze, and fabric. Workmen were needed. Maybe there was a place for his hands in the worship of Yahweh, after all! Oholiab's too. And, to think, he had been on the verge of getting rid of his tools forever!

When the people were dismissed back to their homes, he raced through the camp to Oholiab's tent. He found his friend having just returned from the assembly, playing with his young son. At the sight of Bezalel, Oholiab set the little boy down and strode to meet Bezalel, his face radiant. "Were you there? Did you hear the news?"

"Yes!" Bezalel said. "Moses has called for craftsmen. Are you going to volunteer?"

"Without a doubt!" said Oholiab.

* * *

In the days that followed, Bezalel and Sebia watched with excitement as the pile of treasure grew. It was soon three times the size of the pile of gold Aaron had collected for the golden calf.

Shoshan, Benjamin, and other craftsmen who had worked with Bezalel sought him out and asked if he planned to volunteer to work on the tabernacle. He assured them he did and encouraged them to join in.

A week after Moses had called for the collection of treasure to begin, he called another assembly.

Bezalel put on his cleanest clothes in preparation, hoping this would be the day Moses called for volunteers. He was excited and eager to get to work.

The crowd was already thick when he got there, and soon after he and his family were seated Moses got up to speak.

"I told you at our last meeting about the tabernacle God has commanded us to build. At that time, I also told you that all those who are skilled among you are needed in this project. Today I call for workmen. All who are skilled among you, come. Join me here. Pledge yourself in God's service to make everything the Lord has commanded."

At the word "come," Bezalel leapt to his feet. He made his way to Moses, along with craftsmen and women throughout the congregation. He joined a beaming Oholiab, who had been one of the first to get there, along with Shoshan and a multitude of carvers, weavers, perfumers, and craftsmen of every skill.

When the volunteers had all arrived, Moses addressed the crowd again. "Amongst all these, the Lord has chosen leaders. When I was up on the mountain, Yahweh made it very plain who these people were to be. God has chosen Bezalel, son of Uri, son of Hur of the tribe of Judah, and Oholiab, son of Ahisamach of the tribe of Dan, to lead the project and teach others."

As Moses' words sunk in, Bezalel and Oholiab exchanged shocked glances. They then stood motionless as Moses continued.

"So, Bezalel and Oholiab, and every skilled person to whom the Lord has given skill and ability to know how to carry out all the work of constructing the sanctuary, are to do the work just as the Lord commanded." Turning toward the assembled volunteers, Moses asked, "Are Bezalel and Oholiab here?"

Bezalel and Oholiab stepped from the crowd of volunteers and approached Moses. When they stood before him, he stretched out his hands and laid one on each of their shoulders. Listening with bowed head and closed eyes, Bezalel heard words he had only dreamed he would hear.

"Blessed and chosen are you, Bezalel, son of Uri, grandson of Hur, of the tribe of Judah. The Lord has filled you with the Spirit of God, giving you great wisdom, ability, and expertise in all kinds of crafts. You are a master craftsman, expert in working with gold, silver, and bronze. You are skilled in engraving and mounting gemstones and in carving wood. You are a master at every craft. The Lord has given both you, and you, Oholiab, son of Ahisamach, of the tribe of Dan, the ability to teach your skills to others. The Lord has given you special skills as engravers, designers, embroiderers in blue, purple, and scarlet thread on fine linen cloth, and weavers. You both excel as craftsmen and designers. Go and do the work with God-given skill. His blessing rests on you."

For a moment after Moses finished praying, the crowd was still. Then it erupted in a joyous cheer as Oholiab engulfed Bezalel in a great hug. They both fell on their knees in worship.

EPILOGUE

Then Moses summoned Bezalel and Oholiab and every skilled person to whom the Lord had given ability and who was willing to come and do the work. They received from Moses all the offerings the Israelites had brought to carry out the work of constructing the sanctuary.
—Exodus 36:2–3

Bezalel son of Uri, the son of Hur, of the tribe of Judah, made everything the Lord commanded Moses; with him was Oholiab son

of Ahisamach, of the tribe of Dan—a craftsman and designer, and an embroiderer in blue, purple and scarlet yarn and fine linen.
—Exodus 38:22–23

Moses inspected the work and saw that they had done it just as the Lord had commanded. So Moses blessed them.
—Exodus 39:43

DISCUSSION QUESTIONS

1. Bezalel is depicted as excelling at artistic endeavors from the time of his childhood. How might the talents and interests of children relate to their eventual career choices?

2. In the story, Bezalel's faith in God was eroded to the point where he began following the Egyptian religion. What contributed to this? Are there parallels in our own families and culture?

VIOLET NESDOLY

3. Amulets were thought to provide protection and good luck for Egyptians. Does our society have anything similar? How would we break the spiritual and emotional hold of such objects?

4. Bezalel found his identity in his work. How do we do the same thing? What other things can give us a sense of identity and worth?

5. When the Israelites left Egypt, their long-awaited dream of freedom quickly became its own trial as they exchanged slavery for a nomad existence in the desert. How is this similar to what sometimes happens when we pursue our dreams?

6. God instituted the Passover to commemorate a historical event. What religious festivals or holidays do you celebrate? What do they remind you of? Do you have similar celebrations for family or community events? Share the stories of these celebrations.

7. What did you think of Noemi as a person? As a mother? How is she like or unlike your mother?

8. What role did Oholiab play in Bezalel's life? Does anyone play such a role in your life? How does he or she help you?

9. In what ways did Bezalel's grandfather Hur influence him? Do—or did—you have such an influencer among your family or friends? Who is it? Describe the impact of his or her life on yours.

10. What was your reaction to the Israelites' frequent struggles with grumbling about circumstances and rebellion toward their leaders? What, in your life, is a recurring struggle?

11. "We live our lives forward but understand them backward" is a saying derived from the writings of Soren Kierkegaard. What does that statement say to you?

12. The Bible describes Bezalel as filled *"with the Spirit of God, with skill, ability and knowledge in all kinds of crafts"* (Exodus 31:3). How might this differ from having only artistic talent and natural giftedness?

13. How would you describe the book's theme or message? What effect did the book have on you?